THE DNA OF

ORPHAN
BLACK

THE DNA OF ORPHAN BLACK
ISBN: 9781783297962

Published by
Titan Books
A division of Titan Publishing Group Ltd
144 Southwark Street
London
SE1 0UP

www.titanbooks.com

First edition: June 2017
10 9 8 7 6 5 4 3 2 1

Published with the permission of Boat Rocker Brands
and Temple Street, a division of Boat Rocker Media Inc.

Titan Books would like to thank John Fawcett and Graeme Manson, Tatiana Maslany,
Mackenzie Donaldson and all the cast and crew of Orphan Black who contributed to this
book. Thank you also to everyone at Temple Street Productions and Boat Rocker Media.

Did you enjoy this book? We love to hear from our readers. Please e-mail us at:
readerfeedback@titanemail.com or write to Reader Feedback at the above address.

To receive advance information, news, competitions, and exclusive offers online,
please sign up for the Titan newsletter on our website: www.titanbooks.com

A CIP catalogue record for this title is available from the British Library.

Printed and bound in the USA by LSC Roanoake.

THE DNA OF
ORPHAN BLACK

ABBIE BERNSTEIN

TITAN BOOKS

This Spread: Helena's sniper rifle sight [episode 2.05]
Next Spread: The immediate aftermath of Beth's suicide [1.01]

THE NUCLEUS

THE
CREATORS

Orphan Black *had its genesis in the mid-nineties at the Canadian Film Centre, where John Fawcett and Graeme Manson became friends. "We made a vow that we wanted to do something together," Fawcett explains.*

"We were interested in first-person-told stories," Manson says, "like *Run Lola Run* and *Memento*. We loved those narratives that had a real pace. You're in the shoes of the protagonist, and the protagonist doesn't know what's coming next. Other influences are classic existential sci-fi things that we've referenced in *Orphan Black*, like *Frankenstein* and *The Island of Dr. Moreau*. The breakneck storytelling was influenced by *Breaking Bad*. The more serialized storytelling of *Six Feet Under* and *The Sopranos*, [which] were on TV at that time, mixed with those feature film influences, all brought some DNA to the show."

Fawcett recalls, "In 2001, I pitched Graeme a concept about a girl who basically sees her twin commit suicide by train in front of her eyes."

"And in that moment," Manson elaborates, "the girl sees fear in her doppelgänger's eyes." That, of course, is the opening scene of *Orphan Black*. "My next question was, 'And then what?' And John was like, 'I don't know. That's your job!'" Manson laughs.

In the initial premise, it was a subway train, but, as writer/co-executive producer Alex Levine observes, "It proved extremely difficult to shoot in the Toronto subways, so it ended up on a train platform."

"This was going to be a feature film to begin with, [not] a TV series," Fawcett explains. "We talked about all sorts of different things that this opening scene could present – an alternate reality, a window into another time – but clones definitely came up. We went off and explored every other idea, only to come back to clones. Initially, it was, 'Clones are a cliché. Everything about them is terrible.' That's why we were trying to think of any other answer. We went, 'Okay, [find out what] we've never seen done with clones before, and let's do that.' There's great opportunity for humor, for mystery and conspiracy, for body horror and science. We both wanted not just a show that would keep pulling the rug out from underneath the viewer, but a show that could go from being almost absurd humor to being very emotional and dense and dark, back to being action and kind of lighthearted."

"It seemed like rich territory," Manson says, "and had been under-served. The moment I began to think and research more about clones, and used our science consultant, Cosima Herter, in that respect, I started to get excited about the nature/nurture aspect of the story, the deeper themes and questions of body autonomy."

Fawcett relates, "It languished for a little while, because we literally couldn't figure out how to

Clockwise from This Image: Tatiana Maslany, as Sarah, and Fawcett discuss an episode 1.01 scene. Fawcett and Leda clone acting double Kathryn Alexandre [3.03]. Manson, Fawcett and Maslany, as Beth, shooting episode 4.01

> *"Doing what really good sci-fi does, which is telling a recognizably human story in a fantastical context, and holding a mirror up to current society."*

end it, so we stuck it on a shelf for three or four years, only to come back with this idea of it being a TV series." With a series, "We could tell a far bigger story."

Fawcett and Manson developed the *Orphan Black* series at a television writing workshop back at the Canadian Film Centre. Kerry Appleyard, who is Senior Vice President of scripted programming for Temple Street, the production company that makes *Orphan Black*, then developed the show's network pitch with its creators. "Graeme and John had some key thoughts about where they wanted it to go," Appleyard says, "so we talked extensively about

the themes the concept could explore, fleshed out the characters and came up with story tent-poles for the [first two seasons] and beyond. When you're pitching a serialized show, you have to go into detail, because it doesn't have an obvious story engine, like a police procedural would. We pitched the idea all over the U.S. and Canada. Initially everywhere passed, but then BBC America started ramping up original development and they decided to develop it with us, and not long after that Space, Bell's specialty channel in Canada, jumped on board."

"It was sold as a genre piece," Manson observes, "but we wrote character drama. When you have someone as remarkable as Tatiana Maslany that you can lean on, we were able to let the drama really underpin the genre aspects of the show, so that we're getting something very human, and doing what really good sci-fi does, which is telling a recognizably human story in a fantastical context, and holding a mirror up to current society. I found my original notes from my first meeting with John on the

soon as the discovery, 'I'm not who I thought I was, I'm a clone of someone else, so someone's been lying to me this whole time.'"

Fawcett also had strong opinions about *Orphan Black*'s visual style. "Because the idea of human cloning was so absurd, it was important to me that the show look real. I didn't want it to look like lit sets. In some shows, when you go into the police department, it's really moody and cool, but it's just dark, and it doesn't exist in reality. I came up with a visual style that I called 'dirty beautiful,' because I wanted it to be stylized and beautiful, but have enough grit and edge that I could believe the characters were real people."

In the collaboration between Manson and Fawcett, Fawcett relates, "Because he's a writer, and I'm a director, the way we would work initially is, I'd bring a whole bunch of concepts or images or ideas to him. He'd have his own ideas, of course. He's the one that literally has to write the scripts. Then it comes down to sifting through what we feel tells the story and what doesn't. He's a very good storyteller and I think to some degree over the past four years, not that I'm writing, but I've become a better writer. And in a lot of ways, he's become a better director. We've found a place where we understand each other's job a bit more."

Fawcett didn't know much about real genetics at the outset. "Graeme is more fascinated with the science end of things than I was. He has a very close friend, Cosima Herter, who is a scientist. He kept talking to her about human cloning and what would be involved in that, if it were to happen, how could it happen, and under what circumstances. From back in 2001, 2002, she was feeding us science ideas.'"

Other staff writers also help with the science aspect of the fiction, Manson adds, specifically citing Christopher Roberts.

At the start of each season, Fawcett says, he and Manson go on a retreat together. "We work without anyone else in an attempt to pin down all the big things that we want to do in the season. A whole bunch of ideas have been generated by the previous season. So then you're [saying], 'Okay, well, here's what we had planned for Season Four, and here are all the

concept, dated September, 2001. It's remarkable how much of this did survive. We had Cosima, Alison and Sarah, we had Dyad, we had the cult aspects of Neolution."

Although *Orphan Black* deals powerfully with themes of chosen family versus biological family, Fawcett says, "I don't know that we actually set out to do that. My initial excitement about the concept was that one actor gets to play a whole bunch of very different characters. Maybe that came a little bit from the idea that we wanted to rail against all the clichés that we'd seen in clone concepts before, when there's a thousand drawers in the room, and when you pull out a clone, they're all going to be exactly the same, even their personalities. Graeme and I got excited about the idea that this girl [Alison] was going to be a suburban housewife clone, this girl [Cosima] was going to be a science-y West Coast girl, and Sarah's our punk rock kid who has a small child, and is not a very good mother. That draws you to those thematic elements of identity, of family, of nature versus nurture, of that questioning as

new elements,' and then you start to come up with this blend, and also trying to figure out where our end destination is, and a mid-season climax. Once we've got those, then we'll open the writing room."

"It's a very collaborative atmosphere," says Manson. "There will be six or seven of us [writers], and we will be together months in advance of going into [pre-production]. We'll spend a lot of time looking at where the whole series is going first, and then what this chunk of season needs to do, what the beginning and middle and end are, what's Sarah's main journey, and what each character's journey is. Each story is broken collectively, so that by the time it comes to authorship, when the writer of that particular episode is going off to write, everybody has had their fingers all over the episode. The devil's in the details. Big concepts are great, but then it's endless sweat to get it into manageable drama that actually fits a shooting schedule," he laughs.

Mackenzie Donaldson, who started as

Fawcett at monitor, with Manson (note patch on Manson's hoodie), directing episode 4.10

"My initial excitement about the concept was that one actor gets to play a whole bunch of very different characters."

will usually come back with ideas: 'I would love Alison in rehab.' That was something that he really liked, and Alison performing the musical."

For Season Two, Cochrane recalls, "It was going to be the search for the Original [source of the clone DNA]. We said, 'The Original is going to be S's mom.' But we hadn't sorted out the backstory as to how all of that made sense. It didn't have to be the first thing that we figured out. We had to figure out: how are we going to set up Castor, who are going to be the other players? We came up with the idea of Ferdinand, we came up with the idea of Helsinki."

Cochrane was assigned the episode "Insolvent Phantom of Tomorrow." "I was focused on trying to come up with a backstory for the Original that wasn't clinical. What I didn't want was, 'And S's mom is this doctor who was part of the original experiment.' I felt, because of the nature of the show, we were going to be seeing that kind of character in backstory anyway, so I said, 'She should just be a regular person.' I was excited by the idea that she would be like Sarah, in that she was caught up in this not of her choosing, that she was actually the original victim of the whole experiment.

"I also wanted to make sure that we could find a way to hide her," Cochrane continues, "because [fellow writer] Aubrey Nealon had suggested the idea that she's a chimera [with male and female chromosomes]. We were playing with that unity between Leda and Castor, we were very invested in trying to hide her identity and her gender. So we timelined the whole thing, taking a lot of things that were in place, but also retrofitting to be able to make sure that we're telling the most cohesive, compelling story. I was also concerned that S not know this about her mom, because I didn't want us to get to that moment and feel like we had

assistant to Fawcett and Manson and became a co-producer by Season Four, says, "The plot is so complicated that often first and second drafts can be more plot-oriented than character-oriented. It's [then] just asking the right questions to keep coming back to the characters. The scripts always get there."

Writer/co-executive producer Russ Cochrane gives examples of details. "For Season Two, [Fawcett and Manson] said, 'This is the war between Sarah and Rachel.' And then John

Clockwise from This Image: *Orphan Black* writers' room with (clockwise from bottom left) Will Pascoe, John Fawcett, Karen Walton, Chris Roberts, Tony Elliott, Alex Levine, Cosima Herter. Season Two writers' room whiteboard with story notes. Co-producer Mackenzie Donaldson and Manson. Season Two writers' room whiteboard with different story notes

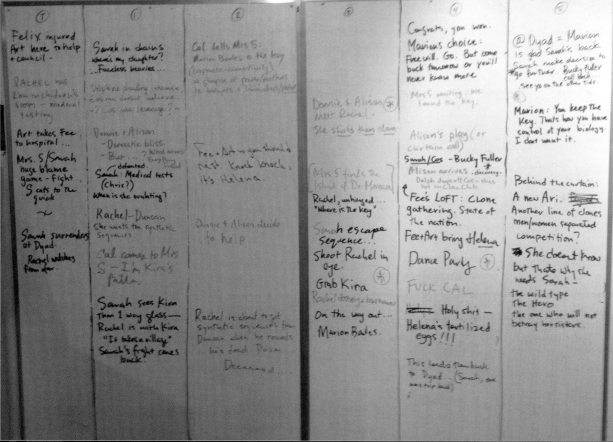

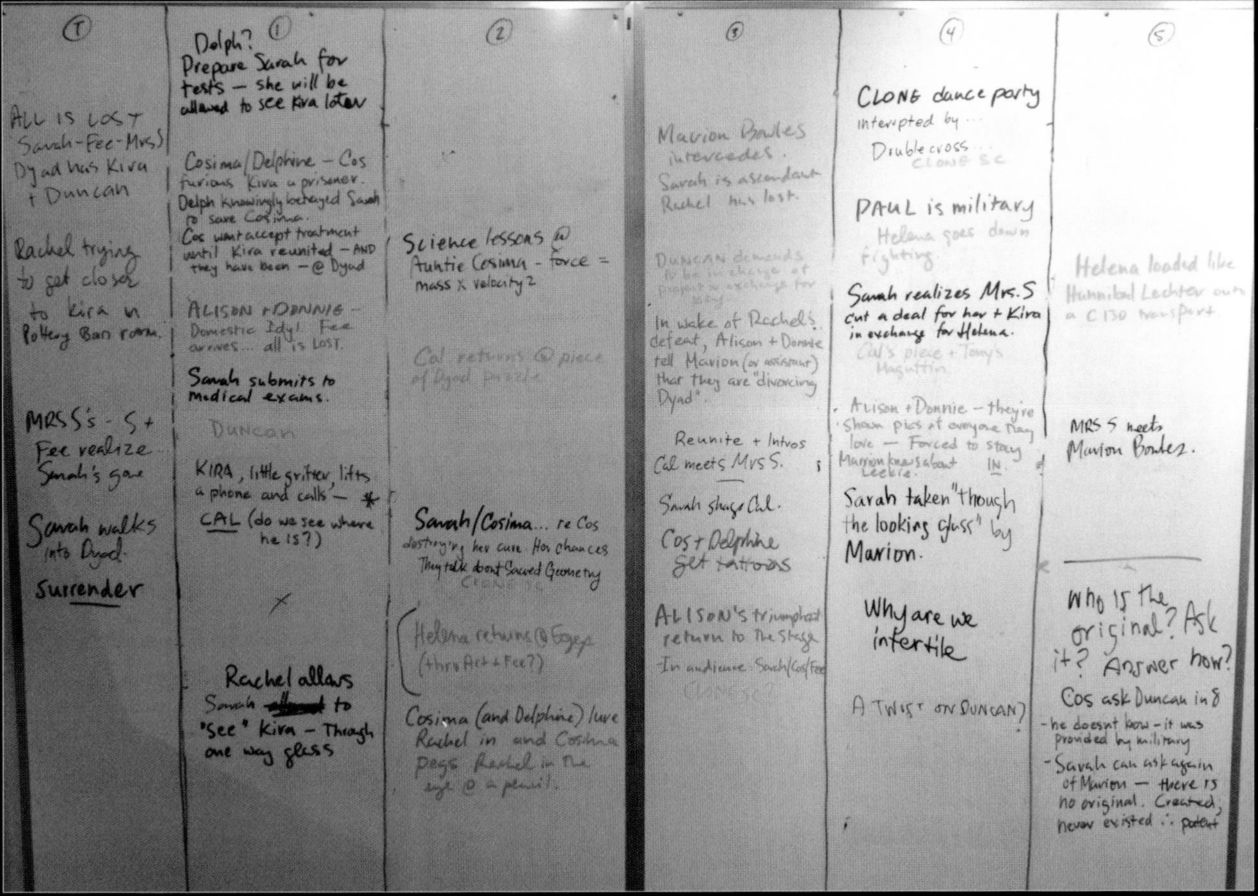

Column T

ALL IS LOST
Sarah-Fee-Mrs S
Dyad has Kira
+ Duncan

Rachel trying
to get closer
to Kira in
Pottery Barn room.

MRS S's - S +
Fee realize
Sarah's gone.

Sarah walks
into Dyad.

Surrender

Column 1

Dolph?
Prepare Sarah for
tests — she will be
allowed to see Kira later

Cosima/Delphine — Cos
furious Kira a prisoner.
Delph knowingly betrayed Sarah
to save Cosima.
Cos wont accept treatment
until Kira reunited — AND
they have been — @ Dyad

ALISON + DONNIE —
Domestic Idyl. Fee
arrives... all is LOST.

Sarah submits to
medical exams.

Duncan

KIRA, little gritter, lifts
a phone and calls — ✱
CAL (do we see where
he is?)

✗

Rachel allows
Sarah ~~to~~ to
"see" Kira — Through
one way glass

Column 2

Science lessons @
Auntie Cosima - force =
mass × velocity?

Cal returns @ piece
of Dyad puzzle.

Sarah/Cosima... re Cos
destroying her cure. Her chances
They talk about Sacred Geometry
CLONE SC

(Helena returns @ Egyps
(thru Art + Fee?)

Cosima (and Delphine) lure
Rachel in and Cosima
pegs Rachel in the
eye @ a pencil.

Column 3

Marion Bowles
intercedes.
Sarah is ascendant
Rachel has lost.

DUNCAN demands
to be in charge of
project in exchange for
baby

In wake of Rachels
defeat, Alison + Donnie
tell Marion (or assistant)
that they are "divorcing
Dyad".

Reunite + Intros
Cal meets Mrs S.

Sarah slugs Cal.

Cos + Delphine
get tattoos

ALISON's triumphant
return to the stage
In audience Sarah/Cal/Fee
CLONE SC

Column 4

CLONE dance party
interrupted by...
Double cross
CLONE SC

PAUL is military
Helena goes down
fighting.

Sarah realizes Mrs S
cut a deal for her + Kira
in exchange for Helena.
Cal's piece + Tonys
Maggitin

Alison + Donnie — they're
shown pics at everyone they
love — Forced to stay
Marion knows about IN
Leekie

Sarah taken "though
the looking glass" by
Marion.

Why are we
infertile

A Twist on Duncan?

Column 5

Helena loaded like
Hannibal Lechter onto
a C 130 transport.

MRS S meets
Marion Bowles.

Who is the
original? Ask
it? Answer how?

Cos ask Duncan in 8
- he doesn't know - it was
provided by military
- Sarah can ask again
of Marion — there is
no original. Created,
never existed ∴ potent

Fawcett holding
the steadicam

been completely betrayed when we had trusted."

Because of the unusual way that *Orphan Black* is made, with one actress playing multiple roles shot with the technodolly, there are production considerations unique to the show. Fawcett notes, "Just by doing the series a bunch, we know where our limitations are. When you get to the actual, 'Here's what we can accomplish in nine days, and here's how much money we have,' inevitably, we wind up having to pull back and simplify in certain areas. At that point, you go, 'Well, this is a hill I want to die on, so if we really want to do this, then we have to prioritize. Something else has got to give.' Sometimes Graeme's priorities are different than mine. But I think we work pretty good together."

Producer Claire Welland, in charge of making sure that everything comes in on budget and on schedule, describes the process. "We have a general production meeting before we go

to camera. The set designer will talk to the production designer. We establish color palettes, and what the various characters' color palettes are. Costume designer Debra Hanson will look at the sets. It's all very much integrated, so no one's working alone. I think most shows work like that."

Of course, most shows don't have *Orphan Black*'s clone issues. Welland relates, "I've never said, 'Could we have less clones,' because this is a clone show, but maybe we'll have to economize in other scenes."

Orphan Black is a challenging series to shoot, but there's no one element that makes it that way, Fawcett says. "The cumulative effect is what makes the show challenging. In Season One, we were trying to figure everything out, because we didn't know what we were doing, so it was a lot more work. But in Season One, we didn't have very much money, we were trying to shoot episodes in seven days, and do all this clone

> *"The real question with these characters is, if in the end they are successful, what do they do with that hard-won freedom?"*

work. We almost killed Tatiana; Graeme and I almost killed each other. After that, it was like, 'We've got to find some other way to do this, so that we can rest Tatiana and not kill ourselves, either.' Fortunately, by Season Two, as we honed the techniques, you know what you're doing from a technical point of view, you just have to figure out the new creative elements. There was a little bit more money coming into our budget, and because we really established the world, we could rely a little bit more on some of our side characters, we didn't have to rely on Tatiana quite as intensely as we had in Season One."

Fawcett points out that he and Manson have cameos in the Season Two premiere. "Graeme and I are shaking hands with Matt Frewer at the Dyad party. We brought our own tuxedos," he laughs.

Orphan Black is very female-centric, with women antagonists as well as protagonists. "We didn't set out to make a feminist show," Manson says. "We knew that the themes were universal, but it was really the women on the show, the female writers, and particularly Cosima Herter, who pointed out how deeply we were examining feminist issues and issues of identity in a layered way. Of course, Tatiana is an outspoken feminist and supporter of LGBTQ rights. So we made a decision to embrace those themes, and I think that putting women at the forefront gave the show its particular humanity."

Orphan Black will end at five seasons. Manson says, "This is a hundred percent our decision and we're glad that the networks are honoring this decision. We had talked about a five-season story for a long time."

Given that one of the reasons *Orphan Black* was made as a television series rather than a movie is because its creators didn't know how to end the film, when did Manson and Fawcett know what

the conclusion would be? Manson replies, "Even when we pitched it to networks, we pitched a loose sort of ending about getting to the top of the pyramid and finding a way to victory and freedom. We began to refer to it as revealing the person that could embody the entire conspiracy [P.T. Westmoreland] and boil it all down.

"The great luxury of this [final] year is, all of the other seasons, we would always have to talk about the end, so by the time we had planned the season, we knew a little bit more about the ending," Manson continues. "But we were always aware that there was only so far down the field we could push that ball. You're not saying, 'How far do we get this season to make it feel like we've taken a huge leap forward in a chapter and learned a bunch of new things, yet the mystery deepens as we go?' That's a challenge every year – knowing vaguely where we're going, but then driving every single character off a cliff, and then the exhausting part of coming back the next season and moving forward again. This year is so much different, because we're coming back and picking up those threads, but at the same time, we're planning exactly where it all ends. And we're finding that process really fun, because we can dig back now into four seasons of mythology. The real question with these characters is, if in the end they are successful, what do they do with that hard-won freedom?"

How does Manson imagine that he and Fawcett will feel when they are finally done with *Orphan Black*? "I think we will be very relieved that we held on to that show that we started in the beginning so blindly, without quite realizing the complexity of everything that we were getting into, but knowing the style of the storytelling that we wanted to have. And then the great feeling of satisfaction that we held onto what mattered and what made the show relevant long enough to grab an audience and tell the story and end the story as we want to. Our little show, our crew, this cast, the writers, John, Tatiana, myself, our director of photography Aaron Morton, and the people at Temple Street. It's such a white-knuckle ride, it's so all-consuming, it's hard to stick your head up in the middle of it and see how it's all going. So taking a breath and looking back will be a good thing."

MULTIPLE PERSONALITIES

For Tatiana Maslany, one difference between the Orphan Black auditions and your average audition was that the actress read for multiple characters. "It was Sarah, Sarah as Beth, and then Sarah, Sarah as Beth, Alison, and Cosima," Maslany recalls. "In the final round, I did an audition that was a marathon of four different clones for all the bigwigs and got to read opposite all the prospective Felixes."

Fawcett and Maslany, as Alison, at an episode 1.02 exterior location

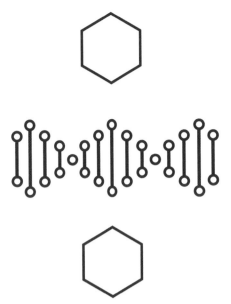

Maslany had originally worked with *Orphan Black* co-creator John Fawcett in 2003, when he executive produced *Ginger Snaps 2*, after directing the original *Ginger Snaps*. Fawcett recalls, "She must have been seventeen, eighteen, and she was playing a thirteen- or fourteen-year-old. She was a very gifted actor – this was a very quirky, strange character that she made completely believable. We stayed in touch after that." The Executive Producers at Temple Street also knew how much talent and potential Tatiana had. They had cast her in two of their previous dramas; in a recurring role on series *Being Erica* (CBC) and as the virgin Mary for BBC's mini-series *The Nativity*.

When *Orphan Black* was being cast, "One of the exciting things about it was the fact that one actor was going to play a whole bunch of different roles," Fawcett continues, "but it's also very terrifying, because your whole series lives and dies on the abilities of one performer. So we spent a lot of time casting. Tatiana was a front runner from the beginning. But I wanted to leave no stone unturned. We cast in L.A., in Vancouver, in Montreal, we even did a little casting for Canadians in England, because we needed a Canadian in the lead role. It was important to our financing; we were a Canadian production, a Canadian network."

When it came down to the last few candidates, Fawcett remembers, "Tat did little things for each of her different characters. She brought eyeglasses for Cosima. I was like, 'That's perfect for that character. We're definitely keeping that.' When we looked at [the other auditioners, it was more], 'Wow, that girl was a terrific Sarah, but I didn't buy her Alison.' Tat was the only one where, [with] each one of her characters, I'm like, 'You know what? I buy all of them.'"

Writer/co-executive producer Russ Cochrane says, "I think Tat wasn't what anybody had originally imagined the character would be like, because when we first meet Sarah, who takes over Beth's life, Beth is a police detective, which means she has to be at least a certain age. Up until that point, Tat had never played anything older than a teenager. Then her auditions were amazing."

On the day of the callback for executives from BBC America and Canadian network Space, Fawcett relates, "Tat rollerbladed in listening to earphones. Most women would be so uptight, they wouldn't want to wreck any bit of their makeup or their look. Tat showed up out of breath, sweaty, and then blew everyone out of the water. Then we saw her perform with Jordan [Gavaris, who plays Felix], and you instantly knew

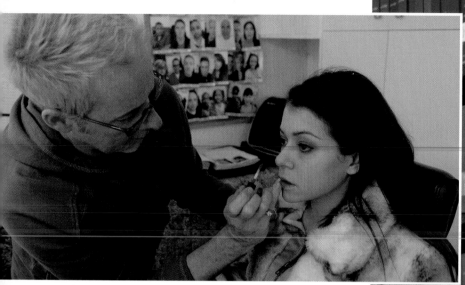

Above: Makeup designer Stephen Lynch applying Maslany's Katja makeup. **Right:** Evelyne Brochu, Fawcett and Maslany, as Cosima, in the library set with some of the crew [1.06]

that that was the combination."

"It was totally magical," Gavaris recalls. "We were the only two actors that didn't get a chance to rehearse [with each other] ahead of time. They tested us all individually first, and then they paired us up together. The auditions with the different Sarah options were always great, these were great actresses. When I entered the room [with] the other Sarahs, we accompanied each other, but Tat was already settled in there. It was the bar scene between Sarah and Felix. I see this girl with this enormous artistic intensity and integrity. She was just so present. That immediately pulled me in and forced me to stop doing my good little actor thing, my 'I'm going to develop the things I rehearsed.' She forced me to respond to her, and she gave me permission to be brave with her. All the other actors [had] stayed stationary, but she got up, collapsed onto the floor and put her head on my leg, I was like, 'I just want to run my fingers through her hair. This is my sister.' It was so intimate and so personal, I completely forgot there were two hundred executives in the room watching us. I thought, 'Oh, we got the parts. Oh, this is real.' She's one of those very rare artists that gives other artists permission to fail, and to do what they want to do."

Maslany is full of praise for Gavaris and her other costars. "We have so many great actors on the show. We're really lucky that everybody's up for the play and the challenge of it, and up for collaboration. I feel like the clones don't exist until I'm across from somebody and speaking to them and they're talking to [Sarah] differently than they would to Alison or than they would to Helena. My scene partners give me all I need to know about these characters and how they're perceived in the world. I think we all know that we're on something that people care about, and we don't take that lightly."

Of her collaboration with creators Fawcett and Graeme Manson, Maslany says, "I trust them implicitly. I'm interested in talking about the things [that affect the characters]. I'm open to being surprised, and I like that. A dialogue helps to clarify things or move things in a different

"*My scene partners give me all I need to know about these characters and how they're perceived in the world.*"

direction, but it's never been like, 'No, I won't do that,' it's more, 'Oh, awesome, can we try that?'"

Fawcett says of Maslany, "I love her. She's so talented, and every day I get to go to work with her, I feel like it's a gift. She's an incredible collaborator. She's for the most part very easygoing. She's willing to try anything and

risk making herself look bad. She wants to be connected in every moment. Some of the spontaneous little moments she's done, those have been the moments that go into the show that fans really remember. She's got this great mindset about the work, because she's done all of the thinking. She knows where the character is supposed to be, but she has nothing set in stone. That stuff is occurring in the moment."

Manson notes, "Before there was Tat, we had some pretty cool characters that popped on the page, but the revelation that Tatiana could pull this off and delineate these characters and make each one of them so distinct, it's given us the incredible ability to write a deeper show. There's

Fawcett and Maslany, as Sarah, on an exterior shoot for episode 2.01

"The characters individually were so well written. Any one of them would have been exciting to play, but getting to play them all was mind-blowing."

never a point where we say, 'I don't know if she can do that.'"

At the outset, Maslany relates, "I don't know what I expected. I'd never read this sort of opportunity for an actor before. The characters individually were so well written. Any one of them would have been exciting to play, but getting to play them all was mind-blowing. I think it was a big learning process for all of us in terms of what we were going to do with it and how far we'd go in terms of having clones, and how complex the clone scenes would get."

Regarding Maslany's contributions to the story process, writer/co-executive producer Alex Levine says, "Tat often has some general thoughts about a script. For example, she might say that Sarah's line feels too procedural, that she wished the character empathized more throughout. That kind of feedback is valuable and we always pay attention."

Maria Doyle Kennedy, who plays Mrs. S, says that playing opposite Maslany's different clones is "mental. But mostly what we get from it is just outrageous respect for Tatiana and what she does."

Kristian Bruun, who plays Donnie, has become more accustomed to playing opposite the different clones as *Orphan Black* progresses. "I love that Donnie is part of the Clone Club, and that he's now open to this world. At first I'd [primarily done scenes] with Alison, and that's the Tatiana that I'm used to working the scenes with. The first multi-clone scene that I worked in was when Donnie discovers that Sarah and Alison are clones. I'd of course seen the show, and all the other versions of her, but to see her off-camera [dressed as a clone other than Alison] really threw me the first few times. The hair and makeup departments do such a stellar job of separating these women, and so does Tat, that it really is off-putting, in the most wonderful way. It makes the acting job exciting and unique, compared to any other that I've had."

Bruun also cites Maslany's work ethic as an inspiration. "Tat works harder than anybody else on this set. The hours that she puts in, the level of performance that she puts out, and the leadership that she humbly [displays] is so endearing and so amazing to work with that everybody wants to do an amazing job for her, not just for the sake of their job the next season – they want this thing to be an amazing piece because of what she does. She really leads by example. It's such a joy to work with her and everybody in the crew, that every chance that I get to be on set is just the happiest day of work ever."

Ari Millen, who plays the male Castor clones introduced in Season Two, says he's learned a lot from Maslany. "It was very easy to get nervous and worry about too much at once, so one of the best lessons I learned from watching Tat work is just watching her breathe through the scene – if you're feeling overwhelmed, take a breath," he laughs.

Actress Kathryn Alexandre has perhaps one

of the most unusual jobs on television – in two-clone scenes, she plays whichever clone Maslany is *not* playing in the shot, both so that Maslany will have an acting partner and so that the technodolly will have a body to capture. In the beginning, Alexandre says, "It was trial and error. I don't think anyone really understood exactly how we were going to do it until we actually got it on its feet. We did have a full day of rehearsal before we started production where we worked with the technodolly, which is the computerized camera that does the clone shots, so that the crew and Tat and I could get used to working with that technology."

It is important that Alexandre match Maslany's performances as closely as possible. Alexandre explains, "When it comes down to the final edit and the visual effects, they tend to use parts of my body and to stick them on her. I focus on how Tat holds herself as each clone. The acting that I'm giving to Tat is what's most important, but in terms of editing of the show, it's really my physicality and whether it matches hers. So

I asked to receive all the dailies, so that I could watch what Tat does every day she's filming, even when I'm not on set. I study where each clone places their weight, which foot they lean on, where their head tends to tilt, what their hands tend to do, how they walk, how they sit, how they run. I'm always coming at it as an actor. It's not just mimicry, and I'm not just focused on what the accent sounds like and how the characters move. I am focused on acting the part, what the characters want in the scene and the emotional core of them."

Maslany and Alexandre discuss nearly every scene, Alexandre adds. "'What is this scene about, what do both of the characters want?' [When] Rachel's never been emotional in a scene before, and then we do the scene where Rachel needs to get emotional, we'll have a conversation about, 'What does it look like when Rachel gets emotional? How far will she go?' Often, when a character's been pushed in a direction that we haven't seen them go before, we try to figure out how they'll react."

Maslany about to demonstrate Helena's passion for food, with camera crew [2.05]

"I feel really lucky that I have such a collaborative relationship, that open dialogue and input with hair and makeup and wardrobe, and with John and Graeme."

For the clones, Maslany says, "I think that was important for all of us to highlight and explore the differences. I've never [before] been so heavily involved in the making of something, in terms of ownership over those characters. I feel really lucky that I have such a collaborative relationship, that open dialogue and input with hair and makeup and wardrobe, and with John and Graeme. It does help for all of us to put in our ideas, so that we don't get stuck in one way of seeing the clones, so that they can continue to grow and change and evolve.

"I think every production [department has] a very specific, detailed vision for each character," Maslany continues. "There was no, 'Oh, we'll put this one's hair up in a ponytail, and this one will have her hair down.' It was, 'Okay, who is this person, how does she see the world, how does she express herself, how does she dress herself?' As you get to know the characters, you continue to deepen them and move them. You can't ever [relax and] sit back."

There are some shots where the viewer can tell which clone is onscreen, even when only a forearm is all that's visible. Maslany opines, "That's a testament to [costume designer] Debra Hanson, who has such an eye for different characters' styles, and Stephen Lynch, who does my makeup. He colors me differently depending on who the clone is, so my skin takes on a different health."

Makeup designer Lynch describes working with Maslany as "a slice of Heaven. I want to give her everything I can to help her, and I think that's my greatest pleasure as a makeup artist in this industry. We'll discuss a new character whenever we have five minutes. If she can look in the mirror and embody her new character, and if I've had anything to do with that, then I'm very pleased."

Seasons One to Three hair designer Sandy Sokolowski agrees, "Tatiana is completely in a class of her own." Sokolowski also notes that Maslany wears a wig for most of her characters. "In the first season, her own hair was being used for Sarah and for Beth – I was straightening it, curling it, whatnot. But between those first two seasons, she got her hair cut off, so it became a wig."

Sokolowski says in his work he's proudest of "the character development with Tatiana, the actual wigs themselves, the amount of work that goes into them, and then sometimes just making the day go seamlessly. When you put those [wigs on Maslany] and see what happens, you feel you have contributed in a positive way to that character."

Hanson explains, "I do a lot of listening to what people think, and then add my own touch to it and go into the fitting room with Tatiana. It's a real collaboration. It's hard to get her for fittings, because she's on camera every day, so the whole prep before we shoot is really important."

When she's asked if her background in improvisation – Maslany is well known for participating in the Canadian Improv Games – helps in crafting the clone personalities, Maslany replies, "Absolutely. When you're doing improv, you're constantly creating new characters. On the spot, you have to physically and vocally embody a new person and take on their world view. That's really helped me in terms of character creation. Also, creating a person who's across from me who's not actually there. Kristian and I, and Jordan and I do a lot of improv in character during the scenes, which keeps it alive and changing and growing. It's really fun. I owe everything to improv. There's so much environment and prop and mime

Fawcett and Maslany, as Rachel, share a light moment shooting the final scene of episode 4.10, with key hair stylist Katarina Chovanec

work in improv. I did it for ten years and loved it so much growing up."

Sometimes improvisations done during filming are used in the final cut, Maslany adds. "As long as it's in character and it's not detracting from the story or moving in the wrong direction, they're open to it. As an actor, to feel like you can contribute like that, that you're being heard and you're in the right voice and saying something that character would say and they use it, that's a huge gift."

In 2016, Maslany won the Emmy® for Outstanding Lead Actress in a Drama for her work in the Season Four *Orphan Black* episode "The Antisocialism of Sex," in which she portrays six of the Leda clones. The actress from Regina, Saskatchewan is the first Canadian in a Canadian production to have won this award.

There are varying opinions on which clone Maslany most resembles in real life. Doyle Kennedy recounts, "Tatiana's real-life mom came on set one time. I was hanging out, chatting to her – real mom and fake mom were bonding – and I asked her what it was like to see Tatiana playing all these different people. She said, 'I guess I most identify Tatiana with Sarah.' I would do the same, probably, mostly because it is more like the way she would dress in real life. Her mum also said, 'When Sarah's not on screen, and some of the other [Leda clone]

characters are, the other clones are interacting, I wonder when Tatiana will be back on.' And that's her own mother in real life! That's how convincingly [Maslany] plays characters. None of the characters are really her, they're all from Graeme Manson's mind."

When asked if she has a favorite clone relationship to play, Maslany replies, "Helena and Sarah, especially when they were discovering their connection and discovering their love for each other. I love that pairing. Alison and Sarah too have a bizarre friendship, but it's like 'you can't pick your family' is how I feel with the two of them, that they wouldn't be friends outside of it. And Beth and M.K. is one that I really enjoyed."

Rachel is sometimes the most difficult clone for Maslany to play, she adds, "But they all sort of go in and out of that. It depends, I guess, on what they're going through."

Of all the topics *Orphan Black* raises, playing the Leda clones has focused Maslany's interest on one in particular. "Body autonomy is something I've learned in a real physical way on the show," she says. "We're constantly exploring the idea of the clones' bodies and their lives not being theirs to own and not being theirs to do with what they will. That's a subject that comes up a lot for me; there's an element of it in being a woman."

STRAND 1: THE CLONES

FACTS + FIGURES

Place of Birth: London, United Kingdom
Date of Birth: March 15, 1984
Gender: Female
Hair Color: Brown
Eye Color: Brown
Height: 5'4"
Portrayed by: Tatiana Maslany
Appearances (season.episode): 1.all; 2.all; 3.all; 4.all

SARAH

FELIX   VIC   BETH ———— PAUL   KIRA

OLIVIER

MRS S   KIRA   ART   DEANGELIS   COSIMA   ALI

DELPHINE   DONNIE

DR LEEKIE

RACHEL

"We always knew that she was the outsider, the black sheep, that she would be the one who's different from the others somehow."
– Graeme Manson, co-creator Orphan Black

Sarah Manning is *Orphan Black*'s central character, a single mother who has grappled with alienation and dabbled in drugs. Once she learns she is a clone, she finds unexpected inner strength fighting to protect her daughter Kira (Skyler Wexler) and her newfound sisters.

Graeme Manson says when he and John Fawcett created Sarah, "We liked the fact that you follow the black sheep into the story. We knew she was living rough and on the run, we knew that she was a mother. We did not write her as an expatriate Brit until we were in business with BBC America. The most difficult storyline is always Sarah's, because Sarah is the spine of the show. When we're building an episode in the writers' room, we have some big concepts, but it always comes down to, what is Sarah doing? That's always the most time-

consuming and difficult part of the story."

Tatiana Maslany observes, "Sarah being working-class London was a big factor in who she was. Her being off the grid and being the wild one, who wasn't monitored the same way that the rest of the clones were, gave her this freedom and irreverence. She's never trusted anyone, because she's grown up outside of any kind of safe, comfortable system. So she needs this distrust. Her physicality says that, her

Clockwise from Opposite: Sarah encountering clone assassin Helena's sniper rifle [2.05]. Sarah on the station platform witnessing Beth's suicide [1.01]. Happy family moment – Cal (Michiel Huisman), Kira (Skyler Wexler), Sarah [3.02]. Sarah pretending to be Beth [1.01]

aggression and her closedness, and her voice is darker and more muted than the rest. She expresses herself with guardedness, yet she's extremely vicious in terms of fighting for the people that she loves. She's an unwilling hero. So I really like to continue to see how dark we can make her."

Kathryn Alexandre, Maslany's acting double, says, "Sarah's very loose, so her center of gravity is low. She's all about the pelvis and the hips. She'll lean forward, but everything is really relaxed and loose on her."

"Sarah has a defiant look going on," makeup designer Stephen Lynch points out. "I think she touches up her makeup when she can. We took a look from the streets, from the influence of her foster mother and her involvement in the punk movement and the anarchist movement. We started with slates and charcoals and deep

matte blacks, and we borrowed some of the colors from Beth's palette, which were more smoky and coppery. I ended up blending the two together, so we now have an eye makeup which is similar to the first season, but it involves some coppery, smoky shimmer. I think [the makeup is] a bit of war paint as well."

Costume designer Debra Hanson says Sarah's wardrobe style evolved in a similar way to her makeup. "The signature outfit has been a black leather jacket and a very tight silhouette. When she started, she was street punk, with torn tights. After she began [impersonating] Beth, her style slightly changed. We were also outside in winter, so it's very practical. She became tight jeans and boots that she could ground herself with. We always have the hoodie and the leather jacket. We also had a coat that was longer, and she would wear the leather jacket underneath

that, so that we layered her up. [For Season Four], we transition her from that leather jacket, becoming a little bit more hip-hop, without being too oversized or over-scaled. So when the layers come off, it's sexy in a different way, and a little stronger. She stays in the very dark colors. It's a little bit more broken down, greys and blacks, and there's some khaki and a tiny bit of color."

Hair designer Sandy Sokolowski agrees that Sarah's look when we first meet her is "street," as she is in fact on the street. "She's a bit of a grifter, and she's a very sad person on the move. I think she's never cared for herself very well. So we had the braids, and that was to simulate some sort of cutaway on the sides. We started with that semi-homeless sort of person, but still, she looks attractive. Sarah started out as kind of punky, for lack of a better word. She gets her identity through little things, like we thought, well, maybe she might have a favorite earring with a feather in it." Even when Sarah settles down, relatively speaking,

Sarah reluctantly confronts Rudy (Ari Millen) on behalf of Dyad (2.03)

"*She's an unwilling hero. So I really like to continue to see how dark we can make her.*"

she still doesn't do much with her hair. "A little conditioner on there, and if she's going out, she might put on some lipstick."

Different actors have differing views of their character's relationship with Sarah. For Jordan Gavaris, the closest bond his character Felix has is the one with foster sister Sarah. "I have two older sisters and it's the bond I'm familiar with. There's so much history there, it's palpable. You put them on screen together, and if they were just to stand and look at each other,

immediately, without speaking, anyone watching them would see the enormous heartbreak and the damage that the nomadic lifestyle has done to them. That is my touchstone, and it just feels like home."

For Kevin Hanchard, the relationship between his Detective Art Bell and Sarah has evolved, because "Sarah has become sort of an embodiment of Beth to him, and he looks at her as a way of potentially redeeming that, of healing that wound or filling that void that is missing

"You want her to be making all of the right decisions... but if it's not challenged, even by her own personality, then it stops being interesting."

from someone who he loved and who he feels he failed. I think there's absolutely no risk of him ever developing the same sort of feelings for Sarah as he did with Beth – he realizes they're two totally different people – but he's been to war with Sarah, he's been in the fires with her, and he continues to bring her along. The proof is in the instances where he has allowed her to play Beth. That's a huge thing, given how he feels about Beth. I think the line was, 'You're just as fierce as she was. You're more like her than you think.' There's something about that that's comforting for him."

In Season Four, writer/co-executive producer Russ Cochrane says, "We wanted Sarah to make some mistakes, to have a dark night of the soul where she becomes flashes of the Sarah from before the show started, the person who was a fuck-up, who made bad choices. She's the heroine of the show and you want her to be making

all of the right decisions, and ultimately, she does, but if it's not challenged, even by her own personality, then it stops being interesting. So we called Tat, and we said that there was something we wanted to do, and in fact, the network also said, 'What if Sarah goes off the rails?' And Tat was really excited."

"The thing that we liked a lot about that is, it felt like a bit of a return to the beginning of the series, where Sarah was on her back foot the whole time," Fawcett recalls, "and things are coming at her, and she doesn't know who the bad guys are. Those elements of having to lie in the moment or make stuff up, and following clues, are kind of what made Season One great. We tried to bring that feeling back in Season Four."

Left to Right: Sarah talks to Paul as she searches for Kira [2.01]. A terrified Sarah is tied up in the shower [2.04]. Sarah is comforted by foster brother Felix (Jordan Gavaris) [4.07]

FACTS + FIGURES

Place of Birth: San Francisco, California, USA
Date of Birth: March 9, 1984
Gender: Female
Hair Color: Brown
Eye Color: Brown
Height: 5'4"
Portrayed by: Tatiana Maslany
Appearances: 1.all except 1.01; 2.all; 3.all; 4.all

COSIMA NIEHAUS

> *"Cosima is an amalgamation of a few people I know, and people we all recognize. She's the quintessential alternative young woman you see on every city street."*
> – Stephen Lynch, makeup designer

ascinated by the science involved, geneticist Cosima Niehaus is the most enthusiastic of the Leda group about being a clone. She is recruited by Dyad after falling in love with fellow scientist and Dyad-assigned new monitor Delphine Cormier (Evelyne Brochu) at university.

John Fawcett explains that Cosima was initially Graeme Manson's creation. "Cosima was based on West Coast friends and an attitude that he knew."

"Cosima is a character I really love a lot," Manson elaborates. "I love her humanity, I love how smart she is. And her tragic love affair with

Delphine (Evelyne Brochu). It's probably the most romantic the show gets, that relationship."

Unlike some series, where lesbian and gay characters have to come to terms with themselves and/or react to disapproval from others, *Orphan Black* presents Cosima as thoroughly comfortable with her sexuality. "The show is so much about identity," Fawcett says. "And it's about diversity, because as we're designing clone characters, we're always going, 'We want this character to be so different from that character, so how do we do it?' Because that's the point. Our clones are very different,

> "I love her humanity, I love how smart she is. And her tragic love affair with Delphine. It's probably the most romantic the show gets, that relationship."

unique people, and they come from very different, unique worlds, and that's the real fun of it. And with Cosima, Delphine is such an important character, so that gives a link there that you wouldn't otherwise have. So it's a great delight for me to see that."

In fact, Fawcett says, "Cosima meeting Delphine for the first time, and going to Leekie's [Neolution – Now!] talk – there was something magical about that episode ["Variations Under Domestication"]. It's my favorite episode [of the first four seasons] that I've directed."

Tatiana Maslany says of playing Cosima,

"We approached her from a very intellectual perspective, because I thought her weapon is her intellect and her sense of humor and her fascination with the world, so I did a lot of reading and studying. She's the lightest of the characters, in terms of probably being the most well-adjusted and the most loved. I think she's been supported her whole life to be who she is, and she has a great deal of pride in who she is, and [she has] an ease in her body. Also, her dreadlocks are very heavy on my head, so my head is always lolling around, so that just became part of her stance and the way she is,

Cosima uses her idiosyncratic laptop to research the Duncans for Sarah, with Felix [2.04]

"Her weapon is her intellect and her sense of humor and her fascination with the world."

Donnie (Kristian Bruun), Cosima pretending to be Alison, Sarah Stubbs (Terra Hazelton) [4.05]

because she's very fluid, very easy."

"Cosima always tends to lean to one side or the other, and her head is tilted," Kathryn Alexandre adds, "and she uses her arms and her hands a lot to speak. And she'll tend to have one hand on a hip, or rubbing her back, something like that, and her ankles are usually crossed as well when she's standing."

Hair designer Sandy Sokolowski reveals that when Maslany's hair has to be changed from one clone's to another's, Cosima is the one who takes longest. "The goal is thirty minutes for any change. Cosima takes thirty to thirty-five minutes. Cosima is the hardest one to do well. I think she wants to put it out into the world she's cool, because she is a nerd, so she wears her hair in dreadlocks. I have to take a little bit of liberty, to have them at least clean enough to be acceptable."

The front of Cosima's hair is actually Maslany's, and the back part is what Sokolowski calls "a cage" with real human hair for the dreadlocks. "We make a three-dimensional

form, a cage, and then we add to that. That allows us to hide the real hair underneath. I put a nylon stocking over the top of the cage, I sew that to make it firm, and then I start sewing my hairpiece to that. You take human hair, you braid it really tight and you boil it for a few hours, and it becomes a nice fill."

Makeup designer Stephen Lynch relates, "I think [Cosima is] very protective of her identity and rarely varies in her makeup application." For eye makeup, "I went toward navy/purple. I thought black might just be a little obvious. I was able to introduce Tatiana to a young woman, Lovina, who I used to teach makeup to at [CMU] College of Makeup [Art & Design] in Toronto. She was actually the inspiration for Cosima's look. She ended up as an extra on our show. She would come to school with that almost street/ kabuki look; very pale, very matte, very obvious liquid eyeliner with the point on the inside."

Costume designer Debra Hanson observes, "Cosima has an individual take on clothes and

Top Left: Cosima is introduced to Ethan Duncan (Andrew Gillies) at Dyad [2.08]. **Above:** Cosima in the lab under the comic store [4.02]. **Left:** Evie Cho (Jessalyn Wanlim) and Cosima operate [4.06]

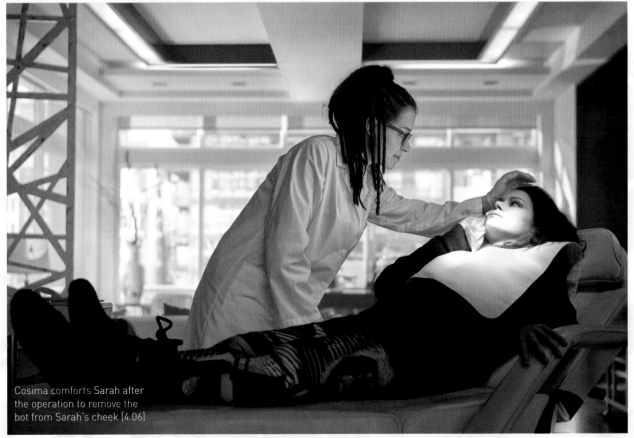

Cosima comforts Sarah after the operation to remove the bot from Sarah's cheek [4.06]

"Cosima is super-smart, but has a heart as big as the ocean."

Cosima with young clone
Charlotte (Cynthia Galant) [4.10]

"Cophine" – Cosima and Delphine
(Evelyne Brochu) are reunited [4.10]

what she wears. It's got pattern and it's got a little bit of bohemian style, and she's ethnically interested. It's slimmer and tighter, but still soft when she's well. When she's not well, it's looser and all about being comfortable. We pull away from the explosive patterning and it becomes more subtle. I call her colors the fall palette, because it's warm and it's earthy, and we try to reflect her global interest in style. It's a little bit eccentric and brave, a very strong sense of taste."

Cosima sometimes wears bold colors, as with her red coat, Hanson adds. "She has a great deal of wines and burgundies and rich, warm colors. She's vulnerable, and yet she's still the one who holds everybody together, very determined, and she has very close friends, and I don't see that so much with the other clones."

When Helena dreams of her "sestras" together in the Hendrix backyard, she envisions Cosima in a Ukrainian folk-dancing outfit. "Nobody admits to whose idea that was!" Hanson says. "It was not mine. It was scripted. When I ordered the real Ukrainian dance costume, Graeme was so excited about it. And so was [Maslany]. She was beside herself. Everybody absolutely loved having that."

Though Kristian Bruun's character Donnie

Hendrix hasn't had many scenes with Cosima, the actor says, "If I had one clone to hang out with, just as Kris Bruun, that would be Cosima. She seems like the most down-to-Earth, funny, nerdy, smart one that I would relate to the most, in my own nerdy way."

Jordan Gavaris feels that, between his Felix and Cosima, "There's an inherent understanding because they're both marginalized, but outside of their sexuality, I don't know how much they've really gotten to know each other."

Kevin Hanchard, who plays police detective Art Bell, says when it comes to which character is most like Maslany, "I'd have to split it between Sarah and Cosima. Ultimately, I think they're all parts of Tatiana Maslany. As any good actor will tell you, any character you play has to be a part of yourself. There has to be some of you in that character. Cosima is super-smart, but has a heart as big as the ocean. One of the great things about Tat is that she cares about everybody in a way that sometimes makes you feel like, 'Oh, I don't do enough,'" he laughs. "It makes you want to be better. So there's that Cosimaness about her. 'Cosimaness.' Let's add it to the lexicon, shall we?"

FACTS ✚ FIGURES

Place of Birth: Scarborough, Ontario, Canada
Date of Birth: April 4, 1984
Gender: Female
Hair Color: Brown
Eye Color: Brown
Height: 5'4"
Portrayed by: Tatiana Maslany
Appearances: 1.all except 1.01, 1.07; 2.all except 2.05; 3.all except 3.05; 4.all except 4.06, 4.10

"Alison was sort of based on my sister
who lives in the suburbs of Calgary
and has her own craft room."
– John Fawcett, co-creator Orphan Black

Alison Hendrix is a tightly wound suburban soccer mom. Married to Donnie (Kristian Bruun), with two (adopted) young children, Alison initially views being a clone as she might a backed-up sink – a nasty inconvenience to be dealt with behind closed doors and never mentioned again – but she eventually feels a sense of sisterhood.

Although Alison is based in some respects on John Fawcett's sister, Fawcett is quick to note that, unlike Alison, "My sister does not have an alcohol or guns problem." Also Fawcett's sister probably isn't a clone. "As far as I know," he jokes.

One reason for creating Alison, says Fawcett, is so that *Orphan Black* can play with a certain type of humor. "Graeme [Manson] and I have a hard time taking ourselves too seriously. Inevitably, the humor finds its way in almost everywhere."

Fawcett adds that Alison is the protagonist in one of his favorite scenes that he's directed, "when Alison tortures Donnie with the glue gun," in "Variations Under Domestication."

Jordan Gavaris says, "The comedian in me really likes Alison, because I get to incorporate my improv background. The Alison/Felix relationship is shiny. It's attractive because it's funny and light, it's a reprieve from the heavy scenes that are recurrent in the show."

Tatiana Maslany relates, "Alison was the scariest [character] for me initially, just because I was like, 'How could I be a mother? I'm twenty-seven, and I've only ever played thirteen-year-olds'," she laughs. "But she was really fun, because she came out of this image of what a soccer mom was to me. She was somebody who sees her life as cookie-cutter, and it was going to be perfect, and then, as things fall apart, she just tries to hold onto them even stronger. I like playing with that exterior totally negating what's actually going on inside.

"She wants to project perfection, and so everything about her clothing says, 'I'm proper, I'm a good woman, and I don't have sex.'" Maslany laughs again. "And these are all lies. She's a murderer, she's pretty sexual, and quite vicious. She's done so many horrible things, and yet she continues to put out this image of herself

Left: Alison, in her signature pink, attends rehab at the New Path Wellness Centre [2.06]. **Below:** Alison's postcard advertising her run for School Board Trustee

TIME TO SCHOOL MARCI COATES.

ELECT
Alison
HENDRIX
SCHOOL TRUSTEE

VOTE FOR ALISON
VOTE FOR CHANGE

"She wants to project perfection, and so everything about her clothing says, 'I'm proper, I'm a good woman, and I don't have sex.'"

Alison, pensive in her own home [1.03

This Image: Alison making a speech in her run for School Board Trustee [3.07]. **Opposite:** Sarah Stubbs, Conrad (Kent Sheridan), Alison, Carter (Carter Hayden), and Kelsey (Barbara Johnston) rehearsing the musical *Blood Ties* [2.01]

"*[Alison's] very together and very matchy-matchy. Everything's precise, and she loves all those pinks and feminine pastels.*"

judgment about what the rest of the clones do, and yet she's mad."

Kathryn Alexandre observes that Alison's body language is very closed off and controlled. "Alison is very upright, and her arms tend to be very close to her body, even if they're gesturing. She tends to stand with her arms crossed, or one hand on her face and her other arm crossed underneath that arm, and she moves very quickly and precisely."

For Alison's wardrobe, costume designer Debra Hanson says, "Alison was Miss Suburban. There's still a lot of that, very together and very matchy-matchy. Everything's precise, and she loves all those pinks and feminine pastels. [In Season Five], she's got a lot of work clothes. She has jackets and she has some skirts now and blouses and she's got a real 'I am an important person on a committee' look."

Makeup designer Stephen Lynch says, "I think Alison is running as fast as she can. Once she has everything in place, whether it's her mascara, liner, favorite lipstick, and her

bangs, and then her house organized, she can breathe a little bit. I think that's why she rarely, if ever, varies her look. It keeps her from flying apart. I think Alison's look is from her happy years in high school, as well. Alison's never changed it. I think she wishes she was still back there. Her color palettes are purples, mauves and bright pinks."

Hair designer Sandy Sokolowski agrees with Lynch about Alison. "A lot of people view themselves and style themselves after the popular time in high school. That's what we were going for. I believe she runs straightener through her hair. The bangs are a little bit left over from when she was in high school. We have done her where she is very prim and proper and polished, and then we try to express how much she's breaking down in her character, just in subtleties, just a little bit off."

After Donnie accidentally kills Dr. Leekie (Matt Frewer), he and Alison bury the corpse in their garage. Art director Jody Clement says the Hendix garage was constructed on a soundstage with this plot point in mind. "We built the garage

"They love their quiet suburban lifestyle. They really cherish it. They love their family, they love their community, they love being leaders of a sort within their community. And Donnie loves Alison, even though they bicker a lot."

set in the studio, but we also had to make sure we could drive a vehicle into the garage, so we definitely had some engineering feats to take on when we built that set. We built it as if we built a real garage out in the real world, with the exception of the floating floor."

The Hendrix backyard, Clement explains, "is built in the studio as well. There are visual effects that are added to it afterwards to create the sky and the clouds. We have high-quality fake grass in the back yard. It actually has [an area] where you can see that little bit of yellowing grass that's shriveling up inside, and we use real paving stones, and then when we change the seasons, we swap out the fully foliaged trees with trees that have lost their leaves."

One of Alison's more memorable moments is when she and Donnie celebrate an illegal financial windfall. Maslany reveals that she and Bruun inadvertently inspired the scene. "Kristian and I one day were just trying to stay warm in a parking lot that we were shooting in, and so we put on some music and started dancing. [Fawcett] was there and said, 'We have to do a scene of Donnie and Alison twerking on the bed, in money.' And so it came out of that."

Bruun, whose Donnie has most of his scenes with Alison, says, "They work [as a couple] on some level. They have had a weird rough patch in the last couple months with this whole sestra thing, with Dyad, with Castor, with all this craziness that has gone on in their world. They love their quiet suburban lifestyle. They really cherish it. They love their family, they love their community, they love being leaders of a sort within their community. And Donnie loves Alison, even though they bicker a lot. I very much think Alison wears the pants, and I think that works for Donnie, he's fine with that."

Maslany says she's also loved Alison's forays into community theatre musicals. "I was like, 'This is my dream come true.' I want to do more of that."

Alison's first musical, *Blood Ties*, was in reality written by Anika Johnson and Barbara Johnston, friends of *Orphan Black* co-producer Mackenzie Donaldson, and Johnson appears on the show as the company piano player, while Johnston is onstage as part of the cast. After Donaldson had helped market *Blood Ties*' run at the Edinburgh Festival Fringe, she suggested it to Fawcett and Manson. "I thought it had about a ten percent chance of them choosing it," Donaldson laughs, "but I thought, 'It's female-led, the music is great, it totally satirizes what's going on in

FACTS + FIGURES

Place of Birth: London, United Kingdom
Date of Birth: March 15, 1984
Gender: Female
Hair Color: Blonde (dyed)
Eye Color: Brown
Height: 5'4"
Portrayed by: Tatiana Maslany
Appearances: 1.all except 1.01, 1.02, 1.05, 1.06; 2.all except 2.07, 2.08; 3.all; 4.02, 4.03, 4.04, 4.09, 4.10

"Helena has this duality in her, this angel and demon, and that was where I wanted to approach her from." – Tatiana Maslany

Raised by Ukrainian nuns, then held by Proletheans who programmed her to see the other Leda clones as abominations, Helena is introduced as an assassin bent on killing her sisters. It is only when Helena encounters her twin, Sarah, that the tormented woman begins to question her conditioning. Now Helena is a formidable defender of her "sestras."

John Fawcett says, "Helena began life as 'Assassin Black.' That's what we called her. Then she became a little bit more like a serial killer. But when it came to, 'She's going to be a character onscreen,' we weren't entirely certain what direction we wanted her to go. Tat made Helena into a much more emotional character, someone we began to sympathize with."

"We knew a lot about the character," Graeme Manson elaborates. "She was the antagonist for the first season, and was revealed to be Sarah's twin and they would come head to head. But we hadn't really developed the character until Tatiana sunk her teeth into her."

When the creators first sat down with Maslany to discuss Helena, "Tatiana said, counter-intuitively to what we were doing, that she felt Helena was proceeding from a place of love," Manson recalls. "She was desperate for connection, it was the thing that was missing for her. All of her violence was from never having love. Helena yearns for family. So that humanized the monster for us – she has an innocent quality that we were then able to write for."

Helena says she was raised by nuns until she was twelve, but then tells Rudy (Ari Millen) that she was forced to shoot a puppy when she was nine. So were those especially mean nuns or is it a continuity glitch?

"No, that's a screw-up," Fawcett acknowledges. "She lived with the nuns until she was ten or eleven, there was an incident where she was provoked and she took out the eyes of Sister Olga. I'm imagining she did that while listening to the song 'Sugar, Sugar.' She was 'rescued' by the Proletheans and then she had to survive in a pen and was programmed by the Proletheans to kill.

"Helena's managed to de-brainwash herself, with help from some of the other clones," Fawcett continues. "She's thinking for herself again. But she's had a horrific childhood. So these things come back at her. She's haunted by things that she's done. She's never going to be normal."

Maslany poses for a Helena hair
and makeup test reference photo

> "*I wanted her to have a connectedness to her body. She's able to pounce at a moment's notice. She knows how to kill anybody. That's her weapon, her training.*"

Above: A Helena wig on a mannequin head. **Right:** Helena the assassin (note the doll's head on her rifle scope) [2.05]

"Helena was a surprise mid-first season to me," Maslany relates. "I wanted her to have a connectedness to her body. She's able to pounce at a moment's notice. She knows how to kill anybody. That's her weapon, her training. Finding the other side of her outside of that training, outside of that single-mindedness, was interesting. And there's been a lot of Helena humor, and that was really unexpected to me."

Some of the humor surrounding Helena comes from her unconventional eating habits. Fawcett reveals that when Helena is impersonating Sarah impersonating Beth in "Effects of External Conditions," Maslany decided to eat a muffin Helena-style and "That spawned all of Helena's eating stuff."

Maslany recalls the subsequent Season One diner scene in "Parts Developed in an Unusual Manner." "Helena's eating like she's never eaten before. I think that she was totally malnourished and everything was withheld from her, so when she gets hold of it, she can't stop, like a little rodent getting into a garbage can. She's the most creature-like of the clones, and really fun to play because of her appetite and her ruthlessness. She has this monster rage inside, and yet she also has this child-like thing, because she's not lived in society, so she sees it with a very naïve, open perspective."

"Helena is incredibly loose, but also slightly reserved in her movements," Kathryn Alexandre notes. "Helena doesn't move unless she needs to. Her arms tend to be behind her back if she's walking, or just straight down beside her. There's not much gesticulation. Then, when she's killing people, it's no holds barred."

Initially, hair designer Sandy Sokolowski says, the design departments were only given the guidance that Helena's look should be "Something Joker-like." Sokolowski and Maslany both have in common Ukrainian heritage, as well as upbringings in Saskatchewan, Canada, so they identified with Helena's background. "Tatiana and I [discussed] what would this girl be like? She's Ukrainian, there's the Ukrainian Greek Orthodox background, and there are iconic [religious] images."

Sokolowski continues, "So we see some church icons on the internet, we're thinking, 'Okay, there's a yellow halo around this character – let's do that with hair and let's make it very angelic.'" Helena's hair is yellow, because she would have tried to disguise herself in a hurry. "She's been constantly on the move and she would have done a bad color job on her hair in a gas station [bathroom]."

Makeup designer Stephen Lynch recalls the same process. "We brought in our history books, and went online, and looked at a lot

"[Scarification]'s such a horrifying image of self-loathing and everything else that comes with self-harming."

of Guatemalan/Mexican religious iconography, and we looked at Renaissance Madonnas as far back as the thirteenth century, because we were fascinated by the duality of nature, of what makes someone a killer. We thought, the yin and the yang, the blonde and the black; we incorporated them both in the hair. I saw Helena as very much otherworldly and not quite set in this dimension. And so I took a liberty and tried to make her look like a fresco [artwork].

"We started with the Renaissance colors, burnt siennas, blood-reds, amber colors, and worked that into her basic complexion and around her eyes, and then I exaggerated it," Lynch continues. "Paintings of the Madonna often had their eyes and cheeks and lips created in that color. I interpreted it in a non-literal fashion. We can explain it through lack of nutrition, and living on the streets, and being a survivor of horrors we can only guess at."

Helena also has the extraordinary scars on her back. "It was suggested initially that she have wing tattoos. I wasn't crazy about that idea," Lynch relates. "I couldn't imagine Helena making her appointment Monday afternoon for tattoos." Lynch thought scarification would be more fitting. "It's such a horrifying image of self-loathing and everything else that comes with self-harming."

He first experimented by drawing on himself in a mirror using a red Sharpie pen gaffer-taped to a dulled knife. After that, Lynch says he repeated the test on co-producer Mackenzie Donaldson, at that time the creators' assistant. "I designed [the scars] and have them made [as prosthetics]," Lynch explains. "Then we apply them and I hand-paint them."

For Alexandre, her favorite scenes are "where two clones will just be able to be sisters. There's a scene of Helena and Sarah in the tent, making shadow puppets, and Helena's enjoying having a sleepover with her sister [in "To Hound Nature in Her Wanderings"]. It was just Tat and I in a tent, with the crew outside, so that was special."

Alexandre even got to make a contribution to the scene. "I played Helena first [while Maslany was playing Sarah]. Helena was supposed to fart. When I farted, Tat laughed, and I improvised in Helena's voice, 'Don't let the bedbugs bite.' Tat and the director liked that, so it stayed in the show."

FACTS ✚ FIGURES

Place of Birth: Cambridge, United Kingdom
Date of Birth: March 31, 1984
Gender: Female
Hair Color: Blonde (dyed)
Eye Color: Brown
Height: 5'4"
Portrayed by: Tatiana Maslany (adult); Cynthia Galant (child)
Appearances: 1.09, 1.10; 2.all except 2.03, 2.06; 3.all except 3.02, 3.04, 3.05, 3.09; 4.all except 4.01, 4.02, 4.05, 4.06

RACHEL DUNCAN
CHARACTER PROFILE

"Rachel was probably one of the scariest clones for me to approach, because of her class and her wealth and her entitlement and her coldness." – Tatiana Maslany

Of all the Leda clones, only Rachel Duncan has emerged as a true villain. Raised first by the Duncans and then by Dr. Leekie at the Dyad Institute, Rachel is a "pro clone," aware of her genetic makeup, hungry for power and not only willing but eager to kill those who share her DNA.

"I was quite scared to play that," says Tatiana Maslany. "I'd never done that before. She's so immaculate – her elegance, her power is so still and quiet. She was somebody who I really looked to John and Graeme and Sandy and Stephen and [Debra] to help me find her. We've really discovered her, I think, as we've gone on these past few seasons. She's fascinating to me. There's something about being raised in boarding schools and in a clinical environment, and how that sort of detaches you from emotion and from empathy."

Kathryn Alexandre observes, "Rachel is quite still, and when she moves, she only moves when she needs to, so it's very specific movements, with her head, with no relaxed looseness to her. It's all very precise."

Maslany has noticed one positive result of the clone's upbringing: Rachel's complexion. "Rachel's skin is glowing from years of having been treated well and having been raised in a bubble."Makeup designer Stephen Lynch describes Rachel as "The ultimate high-end woman. On her, I use La Prairie and Chanel and all of the high-end brands. Money is no object. Again, armor, the face she presents to the world – very important. It is diametrically opposed to Sarah's approach, certainly to Alison's. I think Rachel would consider those clones very vulgar. Her statement with makeup would be a non-statement; immaculate skin, polished, perfected, almost a no-makeup look, except for her statement lip. It's very much about class, as well. She represents a certain class in Britain, and wouldn't condescend to obvious effects of liner and vulgar eye-shadows."

Hair designer Sandy Sokolowski says of Rachel's haircut, "You want it to speak for itself, you want it to look expensive, and certainly there's a layer, and a beautiful color. She's the real deal, and she's got great taste, and she's got money, so she has great skin care, great hair."

Costume designer Debra Hanson says, "This feeling of being part of the establishment is really important to Rachel. It's all power, and [her outfits are] all black. She's very mysterious. You think she's evil, but is she? She's so damaged, and you see her struggling with all the things that have happened to her, and struggling with her own conscience. Then later, there are blacks and creams, but it's neutral. It's a sleek simplicity. There's nothing frilly, there's nothing overstated. And strong. Certainly no pastels. And there's that confidence of it. For her, it is close to the body, extremely 'power suit.' Again, the silhouette is

"*Money is no object... Armor, the face she presents to the world [is] very important. It is diametrically opposed to Sarah's approach, certainly to Alison's. I think Rachel would consider those clones very vulgar.*"

Proclone Rachel in her immaculate Dyad environment [2.07]

Clockwise from This Image: Rachel, taking in the view from her Dyad office [1.10]. Rachel with the kidnapped Kira [2.10]. Rachel showing her father Ethan Duncan images from her childhood [2.10]. A wounded Rachel and a furious Felix [3.06]

always something that I'm looking at."

Though it was cut from the aired episode at the end of Season Two, Kristian Bruun's first scene as Donnie opposite Rachel was both intimidating and a landmark for the actor. When Dyad starts to bear down on the Hendrixes, Donnie tries to reassure Alison and resolve the situation by going to Rachel's office and demanding that she leave his family alone, only to have Rachel blackmail him without breaking a sweat. "That was the first time that I ever worked with another clone," explains Bruun, "and so that was really unnerving for me, because it was my last day [of shooting] on Season Two, and here I was working with a different Tatiana, essentially."

After Sarah shoots Rachel in the eye with a pencil in "By Means Which Have Never Yet Been Tried" and Rachel is in the care of Susan Duncan (Rosemary Dunsmore), her adoptive mother, "There's a richness to her," Hanson adds. "It's still neutral, but it's a softer kind of look for her. The thing is to keep her sleek, expensive and neutral, because you just don't know about her. If she's interested in a man, for instance, I'm not going to put her in red, I'm just going to keep her really elegant, but neutral, and steely. We did some underwear for her, and it was steel grey, so it's very sexy and it was hard-edged."

Jordan Gavaris said he surprised himself in the "Certain Agony of the Battlefield" scene where

> "She's so damaged, and you see her struggling with all the things that have happened to her, and struggling with her own conscience."

Felix confronts Rachel. "There have been things like his violence, and his aggression, that I didn't anticipate. That scene with Rachel, when he comes into her hotel room and he paints on her eye patch. On the page, it could have been funny and kind of silly, but then when we went to shoot it, I was just overwhelmed by the amount of rage and aggression and violence that I felt towards this woman, and you just go with it. Obviously, Felix has nothing but disdain for Rachel." However, Gavaris thinks that afterwards, "He regrets it a little bit, because I do."

There are moments when we feel for Rachel, John Fawcett notes. "Because of the way we had seen Helena start life as a villain, and then kind of turn into someone that we could actually sympathize with, even though she was doing some weird, bad things, we understood her and felt sorry for her. Those were things that we wanted to bring to Rachel as well, just to humanize her. But she definitely started off in the world as 'Evil Bitch Rachel.'"

FACTS + FIGURES

Place of Birth: Sudbury, Ontario, Canada
Date of Birth: May 5, 1984
Gender: Female
Hair Color: Blonde (dyed)
Eye Color: Brown
Height: 5'4"
Portrayed by: Tatiana Maslany
Appearances: 3.01, 3.08, 3.10; 4.05, 4.06, 4.10

She started as a bit of a joke, [but we began] finding out what is beneath that heavily made up, nails done, hair done veneer, and bust through that stereotype in a way.

"*She's not a brain surgeon. She's got a little bit of money, but she's spending it on [shopping], and she watches television, and enjoys the celebrity shows.*"

This Image: Krystal talks to Art [4.06].
Above: Krystal tells Felix what she knows about Van Lier and Delphine [4.10]

TONY SAWICKI

CHARACTER PROFILE

FACTS + FIGURES

Place of Birth: Cleveland, Ohio, USA
Date of Birth: March 31, 1984
Gender: Male
Hair Color: Brown
Eye Color: Brown
Height: 5'4"
Portrayed by: Tatiana Maslany
Appearances: 2.08

"[Tony] was very comfortable in his own skin and boldly himself and had no judgments about himself or his gender identity."

Tony's monitor Sammy (Bishop Brigante) tells him about Beth before he dies (2.08)

Tony Sawicki is a transgender Leda clone who shows up in Season Two's "Variable and Full of Perturbation" looking for Beth – and prompts Felix's line, "Holy Tilda Swinton" – after his best friend is murdered.

John Fawcett says, "Because the show is so much about identity, we felt it was important to be as diverse as possible. When we discussed it with Tatiana, it was something that she got very excited about and wanted to be as real about it as possible."

Tatiana Maslany relates, "Tony was a great collaboration between myself, [makeup designer] Stephen Lynch and [hair designer] Sandy Sokolowski. We really wanted him to be his own person and not like the other clones in terms of personality. That he'd grown up in a different environment, a little more working-class, and yet had one great friend in his life who'd supported him. He was very comfortable in his own skin and boldly himself and had no judgments about himself or his gender identity. Even to discover that he's a clone doesn't really faze him; it's just another part of who he is, like, 'Oh, okay, that's a new piece of me that I can take in.' He's done all the soul-searching already. His identity is his. He has a great deal of ownership over it."

"Tat used ankle weights for Tony," Kathryn Alexandre notes. "That gave her a bit more of a feeling of just having more weight on her lower body, so that's what I played with as well. I didn't have the actual ankle weights, but just that feeling of heaviness in the lower body, and have a broadening of the chest to get more of that masculine frame."

FACTS + FIGURES

Place of Birth: East York, Canada
Date of Birth: April 1, 1984
Gender: Female
Hair Color: Brown
Eye Color: Brown
Height: 5'4"
Portrayed by: Tatiana Maslany
Appearances: 1.01; 3.06; 4.01, 4.02, 4.06, 4.07

"[Beth has] a real danger and a darkness to her, and it's singular in terms of not wanting other people to help her or save her." – Tatiana Maslany

While Sarah Manning is the main protagonist in *Orphan Black*, it's Beth Childs who actually sets the plot in motion. If the unhappy police detective had not tried to discover the secrets of Dyad, only to despair and throw herself in front of a train, there would be no life for Sarah to adopt, no trail for her to follow, no path for her to find and fight for her sisters.

"Beth is a mystery in the first season," Tatiana Maslany offers. "We only saw her in a little video footage when Sarah tried to impersonate her, we only got clues to her life through what people said about her. But Beth is one of the most complex clones that I've gotten to play yet. Beth was a challenge. She was new and didn't have an accent or anything, so there was

nothing I could really grab onto in terms of that. It was more just, 'Okay, who is this woman? How do I differentiate her?' She's almost the right side of the law, and yet she's a bad cop," Maslany laughs. "She's her own person in a big way. Her veneer is clean and direct, and yet we like to break her down and make her look exhausted and wary and beaten-down and like she's carrying the weight of the world on her shoulders. She's definitely got a masculine side to her and a strong feminine side to her, too. I like playing with that duality."

"She's a police officer," hair designer Sandy Sokolowski observes. "We see her sometimes with the hair down." She could have had a ponytail, but "We didn't do that, because we didn't want to mix Alison up with Beth."

Beth commits suicide [1.01]

"Beth is a mystery in the first season. We only saw her in a little video footage when Sarah tried to impersonate her, we only got clues to her life through what people said about her."

Makeup designer Stephen Lynch explains, "Each clone has a different [look]. I'll start with a lot of contouring and highlighting. Sarah's a little more lean and mean, and Beth was a little more cut [in terms of muscle definition] in her face, because she's a runner."

Due to Beth's drug use, Lynch adds, "I tried to make Beth in the flashbacks look a little more bloated and unhealthy. Maybe no one else sees it, but it's something I can do for Tat, [so] she can see it when she looks in the mirror – she knows [her character's] face so well. It's just contour and highlight, a little around the mouth, eyes sagging a little, making her a little lighter and puffier up top, so it's enough to fool people that she's all right, but if you look closely, something is off. Her upper lids are heavy and they're a

little puffy. That's really old-school painting with contour and highlight, light and dark."

Co-producer Mackenzie Donaldson reveals why Beth's history is so prominent in Season Four. "That's always been something [John Fawcett and Graeme Manson] wanted to do, a season that had lots of flashbacks to tell that particular story, even though it's an extremely hard and ambitious thing to do, as we've learned," she laughs. "What better character than Beth for us to go back and explore what led her to that [end], and what did she know? It became clear that Beth was the perfect clone to take us back, because we didn't want to go back to 1976 or something like that, when [a clone played by] Tat wouldn't be in the show. It had to be a recent flashback for it to work for us."

KATJA OBINGER

CHARACTER PROFILE

"A wig was made. The hairdresser wanted it dyed and colored, because the clones are genetically identical, so it had to look very obvious, and she had to be ill."

Katja Obinger is a clone from Germany who survived a massacre of Leda clones in Helsinki as a teenager and escaped the assassin Helena in Europe, only to be killed in Canada by Helena's sniper bullet. When Katja tries to contact police detective Beth, it's Sarah Manning, impersonating Beth, who agrees to a meeting. Believing she is talking to Beth, Katja reveals the existence of the clones to Sarah and that they're in danger – a fact proved when Katja is shot dead in front of Sarah.

Although Katja's role was relatively limited in the series, John Fawcett reveals that she was one of the characters used in the auditions. "[Tatiana Maslany] demonstrated her German accent, which she was quite proficient at."

Kathryn Alexandre also played Katja in the auditions. "I was an actor who the casting department hired to just read with other actors for auditions. I read with Jordan Gavaris for his first audition for Felix. Once they cast Tat, then I got a call to audition for [her] double. So me and a few other girls prepared as if we were auditioning for Sarah, Alison and Katja. We did our own interpretations of the clones, because they wanted to make sure that they were casting an actor who could actually have some ideas and play the roles and really give something for Tat to work off of. I had a callback with the director, and then I had a third audition where they brought Tat in, and the two of us played off of each other."

Makeup designer Stephen Lynch recalls that the first two-clone scene that was shot was the Sarah and Katja interaction. "So we needed a full day of rehearsing that before we even started shooting the show." For Katja, "A wig was made. The hairdresser wanted it dyed and colored, because the clones are genetically identical, so it had to look very obvious, and she had to be ill," as it appears that she was suffering from the respiratory illness that afflicts some of the clones, "so we just came up with a look on the fly."

"*We use Skype calls and phones, just so we can shoot in the time we have.*"

Jennifer Fitzsimmons was treated at Dyad for the respiratory illness that also affects Cosima and some of the other Leda and Castor clones. We only see the living Jennifer in clips from her video journal. Delphine (Evelyne Brochu) shows Cosima Jennifer's corpse so that they can better study the disease.

In fact, as executive producer Kerry Appleyard explains, onscreen computer videos and Skype calls are ways to shoot scenes that, literally speaking, have multiple clones in them, but don't require Tatiana Maslany to play two clones in the same shot, which is time-consuming. "We write the scripts according to the [creative vision] and get the story working," Appleyard says, "but then we really have to also do a pass or two to make it work for production, and try as best we can to film it. We use Skype and phone calls, just so we can shoot in the time we have. We have a format that enables us to shoot the show."

DANIELLE FOURNIER, ARYANNA GIORDANO, JANIKA ZINGLER

"Those [clones] weren't as polished – we did think them through, but they were never going to be characters that would be onscreen."

Danielle Fournier of Paris, France, Aryanna Giordano of Rome, Italy and Janika Zingler of Salzburg, Austria are all Leda clones believed to be dead by the time *Orphan Black* begins. Their files indicate that all of them died on separate dates, in separate incidents, in 2012. Even so, we see photos of the young women. Their different nationalities are a testament to the worldwide reach of the Leda project.

Makeup designer Stephen Lynch remembers, "We did some prop shots for clones who are only seen in photographs, the Europeans."

Hair designer Sandy Sokolowski elaborates, "It was a mad dash during the camera tests, so we just did a whole bunch of things in an afternoon. They used it for all kinds of passport or police photos. Those [clones] weren't as polished – we did think them through, but they were never going to be characters that would be onscreen."

Left: Cosima watches Jennifer's video diary [2.03]. **This Page:** The passport photos of (top to bottom) Danielle, Janika, Aryanna [1.02]

FACTS ✛ FIGURES

Place of Birth: Helsinki, Finland
Date of Birth: April 22, 1984
Gender: Female
Hair Color: Brown
Eye Color: Brown
Height: 5'4"
Portrayed by: Tatiana Maslany
Appearances: 4.all except 4.03, 4.05, 4.09, 4.10

"*I liked the idea of a scarred teenage slightly Asperger's-y type clone who survives Helsinki and changes her name and her identity to stay alive.*"

Inset Top: Beth visits M.K. in her trailer [4.01].
Inset Above: M.K. threatens vengeance by fire [4.04].

M.K., aka Mikka, real name Veera Suominen, is a Finnish clone who is evidently the sole survivor of a massacre in Helsinki. She is secretive and reluctant to trust even her fellow clones.

John Fawcett explains M.K.'s genesis. "I had come up with the idea that I was going to develop this new [Orphan Black] comic book series, based on past events of Helsinki, which would be about a clone genocide that happened in 2001. It was going to have a whole bunch of new characters in it and be like a teen clone Breakfast Club, because they'd all be teenagers. And it was all going to end basically in a Red Wedding [massacre]. So it was going to be five issues, Ferdinand was going to be in it, Rachel was going to be in it, and then we needed to invent a whole bunch of new characters. One of the new characters is Veera Suominen. I said to Graeme, 'I've got this idea for the comic book series with this clone who has been burned because, when she was seven or eight, she was in that lab fire that supposedly killed Susan and Ethan Duncan.' I liked the idea of a scarred teenage slightly Asperger's-y type clone who survives Helsinki and changes her name and her identity to stay alive."

Tatiana Maslany observes that, because of M.K.'s devastating early life losses, "She reverts to a very childlike expression. She [feels] safer alone than she is connecting with people. She dresses like a teenager, like when she lost her best friend when she was seventeen [in the Helsinki massacre]. She hasn't moved past that time, physically, in terms of how she stands, how she lives, how she walks around, how she dresses herself, how she looks facially and hair-wise, and how her voice sounds. Also, there was just something so beautiful about the Finnish dialect. I think it's gorgeous and musical and there's something percussive about it, too."

"M.K. is very insecure about the burn on her face," Kathryn Alexandre says, "so although she moves quickly and precisely, she's very contained and everything is inward. She's trying to hide at all times, so her shoulders and her

"She's trying to hide at all times.... She's always a little uncomfortable."

neck are a little slouched. Her hands tend to be rolled up in her sleeves, and her feet tend to be shifting or just a little angled. She's always a little uncomfortable."

Makeup designer Stephen Lynch elaborates, "M.K. has great social anxiety and twitches and hides very much behind her hair. We all know someone like her. She's grown her hair over her scar on her face and we rarely see it. We figure she basically doesn't use cosmetics. She's hiding from the world. So that was an interesting challenge, too. Her nerves manifest themselves through biting her cuticles, and you'll also see some patchiness on her skin and some breakouts around her nose, signifying this anxiety. She has a little more wiry, untamed eyebrows. I color them a bit and use a fixative to keep them in an unruly place. She's wearing a darker wig. It's amazing how young she appears.

"I make the scar myself," Lynch continues, "and I actually put it on Tatiana every time she plays M.K. Even though we [seldom] see it, Tatiana always wants to feel it and know it's there. And I think it also helps that if the camera sees [that area of her face], we know we can use that shot."

Left: Fearful, isolated clone M.K. checks on Beth [4.02].
Right: Beth hugs M.K. goodbye [4.02]

"Just one. I'm a few.
No family, too. Who am I?"

"They're struggling, they're trying something on – they're not embodying themselves, they're putting on an act and they feel exposed."

Opposite: Sarah's improvised impersonation of Alison [2.07]. **This Image:** Dr. Ian Van Lier (Scott Wentworth), Mrs. S (Maria Doyle Kennedy), Sarah-as-Krystal [4.10]

The *Orphan Black* creators, design team and Tatiana Maslany come up with exquisitely distinctive and different personas for each Leda clone. This makes it possible for attentive viewers to pick up on what's happening when one Leda clone impersonates another.

This happens frequently when Sarah impersonates Beth at the start of Season One. Later, Sarah also impersonates Alison (on the fly, twice), Rachel and Krystal. Rachel impersonates Sarah and Krystal. Krystal is made up (without her consent) as Rachel. Alison impersonates Sarah several times. Cosima impersonates Alison. Helena impersonates Sarah impersonating Beth, and later impersonates Alison.

Maslany says with a laugh, "Those scenes always are a total mind-fuck! I never feel like I've got it in those scenes. I think that's not a bad thing, necessarily, because that's where

those characters are at, too. They're playing, they're struggling, they're trying something on – they're not embodying themselves, they're putting on an act and they feel exposed and they feel that they're screwing up and like they're going to be caught out and they're going to be seen as a fraud, and that's everything I feel when I'm doing those scenes. And it is technically so confusing, but that's what is so fun about those scenes. I just love them, they really thrill me."

Maslany adds that she likes the little touches that indicate something isn't quite right. "It's fun for all of us to be off with it a little bit. This is Sarah's version of Rachel, so it's not as impeccable and not as pristine and not as elegant. She struggles to walk in her shoes, her hair's not quite right, she's not comfortable in her skin. And Alison [as Sarah] is a little too clean, a little too community theatre. Her hair

Donnie with Helena-as-Alison [4.03]

is curled in a very done way and her makeup's a little too stagey. So it's fun to play with those little mistakes."

Hair designer Sandy Sokolowski says, "When Sarah was imitating Rachel, that's not even the Rachel wig. That [disguise] wig had bangs on it. We couldn't give her the regular Rachel wig, because that would be a giveaway. [The disguise wig] was a little bit bigger. Sarah was able to put her fingers up and take it off [onscreen], and her hair flows underneath. The real Rachel wig is so exact-fitting that you could never do that."

Sarah's impersonation of Rachel, "As performed by Felix (Jordan Gavaris), through his eyes and his hands, that was great fun," makeup designer Stephen Lynch recalls, "because he made her even more über-fashion bitch than [the real Rachel] could. He took the eye makeup 'up' just a little bit. It's a little more arched and a little more smoky, because it's a look he likes."

Another example of a disguise deliberately

not being quite right, Sokolowski says, is "When Alison is being Sarah, [she tries] to get rid of her bangs. That wig, with Alison's bangs trying to be scrunched in and forced a little bit, there are a lot of layers going on there. You realize that isn't Sarah, but you could see where somebody who didn't know Sarah might [think it's her]."

Lynch says that the clone impersonation sequences are "one of the great joys" of doing *Orphan Black*. "We have to decide how to interpret the other clone's makeup through this person's eyes. Alison impersonated Sarah [when she] went to Mrs. S's house with Felix, so Felix would have done her makeup. 'I know my sister better than anyone, and in fact, I can do it far better than she can.' So I used Sarah's eye makeup, but as applied more deftly and in a more fashion-forward sense by Felix. I always say to Tatiana when we're doing these things, 'I don't care if none of the critics notice, but there will be some viewers who will. You will know it

Ferdinand (James Frain) with Sarah-as-Rachel [3.01]

when you look in the mirror. I want you to see both [clones].'"

Felix also helps disguise Cosima as Alison on short notice. "Cosima is not familiar with that look at all," Lynch explains, "but just took her own eye makeup down and was able to get an appropriate lipstick."

When Helena impersonates Sarah impersonating Beth at the police station, Lynch says, "That is mostly wardrobe and tucking her hair up, and Tatiana did that one on her own. I can't take any credit for that. That is her acting genius on display, not makeup."

When Rachel makes her escape from Dyad by disguising herself as Krystal and making a drugged Krystal appear to be Rachel, Lynch explains, "I painted a bit of her upper contouring and changed the shape of her face slightly, because we don't want to lose who that person is. It's tough when we do no-makeup looks. We still have to incorporate a tiny bit of their look somehow. Otherwise, it just looks like a scrub-faced Tatiana Maslany, rather than looking like Rachel in a hospital or Krystal in a hospital."

Although no one in the *Orphan Black* storyline has so far impersonated Helena, Lynch reveals with a laugh that, "My Halloween costume on set last year was Alison disguising herself as Helena. I had cowboy boots, a dirty, ragged wedding dress, the wig, and the Helena makeup, but I figured, this is Alison, and she just can't resist touching up the eyes. So I used her purple liner and mascara on top of Helena's look, as well as her favorite poppy pink. It's rather horrifying, I can tell you."

In Greek mythology, Leda is a woman raped (in some versions, seduced) and impregnated by a swan that is the Earthly manifestation of the god Zeus. According to the myth, on the same night, Leda also lay with her human husband. She subsequently gave birth to four children, some mortal and some immortal: Helen, Clytemnestra, Castor and Pollux.

Alison Steadman as Kendall Malone,
the "original" of both clone lines [4.02]

Ethan Duncan talking urgently with Sarah [2.06]

n *Orphan Black*, the Leda clones are the result of a metaphorical mating between the substance of a human woman and the god of science.

By the end of Season Four, it's hard to be sure of the origins of Project Leda – or Project Castor, the Dyad Institute, et al – because of revelations regarding still-living Victorian scientist P.T. Westmoreland, author of Neolutionism bible *On the Science of Neolution*.

What we do know is that Professor Susan Duncan (Rosemary Dunsmore) found Kendall Malone (Alison Steadman), a "chimera" with male and female DNA; the male DNA is from a male twin Kendall absorbed while still in the womb herself. Susan Duncan coerced Kendall – Siobhan Sadler's (Maria Doyle Kennedy) biological mother – into letting her take her genetic material. She then collaborated with her husband, Dr. Ethan Duncan (Andrew Gillies), to create the Leda and Castor clone lines.

Graeme Manson explains why the scientists wanted one original donor for both lines. "Kendall Malone's biology was unique. Not only was she a chimera, but within this unique biology, her cells were very regenerative, much like a HeLa cell."

In the real world, HeLa cells were taken from a tumor in Henrietta Lacks in 1951, and were the first immortal human cells ever grown in culture. In 1955, these became the first human cells to be successfully cloned. "Her cancer cells were discovered to be perpetually replicating," Manson continues. "Every cancer researcher, to this day, studies the same set of cancer cells. So that was our concept, a woman whose cells make cloning easy by pure mathematical chance. [The *Orphan Black* scientists] got their cell lines, worked on them, solved some key problems, and had to add certain synthetic sequences to the genome. Those synthetic sequences, in terms of creating experimental humans, are the elements that are making the girls sick, because the genome was tinkered with."

There are multiple purposes behind the creation of the Leda clones. The Neolutionists,

Charlotte Bowles, the youngest of the Leda clones (4.03)

as Leekie, et al call themselves, are interested in creating a superior species of human via genetic manipulation. The Dyad Institute has also patented the clones' gene sequences, which could be legally interpreted to mean that the clones are owned by Dyad. However, in *Orphan Black*, the assumption is that since humans cannot legally own one another in most nations, and the clones are essentially human, any attempt to enforce this through the courts would result in a groundbreaking legal case.

The Duncans raised Rachel as their daughter until age eight. When the Duncans separately faked their deaths in a lab fire, Rachel was taken by Leekie into Dyad and trained to become an executive there. Other Leda clone embryos were placed with women who thought they were participating in conventional infertility treatments. Amelia (Melanie Nicholls-King), carrying twins, was told she was a surrogate, but suspected something was wrong. She gave one baby, Helena, to the church and the other,

Sarah, to the U.K. state. When they encounter one another in "Endless Forms Most Beautiful," the adult Helena kills Amelia for – as Helena sees it – betraying her.

Unlike their "sister" clones, Sarah and Helena are both fertile, even though the Leda clones were all designed to be sterile. Sarah is the mother of young Kira (Skyler Wexler), whose father is Cal Morrison (Michiel Huisman). Throughout Seasons Three and Four, Helena is pregnant with twins, after being forcibly impregnated by sperm from Prolethean leader Henrik Johanssen (Peter Outerbridge). Helena uses fertility instruments employed on farm animals to kill Johanssen. Despite being a loving mother to her two adopted children, Gemma (Millie Davis) and Oscar (Drew Davis), Alison is troubled by her infertility.

Cosima Niehaus – named for *Orphan Black* science consultant Cosima Herter – isn't concerned about her infertility as she is struggling with the more urgent issue of the potentially fatal illness caused by the Leda genome alterations.

Susan Duncan (Rosemary Dunsmore) at home with adopted daughter Rachel [4.07]

> ## *"There's a fundamental human hubris in trying to play God. [Orphan Black] has that element. It's [also] got the banality of evil..."*

Charlotte (Cynthia Galant), the only member of a new generation of Leda clones, also suffers from this illness, which has already killed several of the older generation.

Dyad's sister company BrightBorn, also owned by Dyad Corp., is working on germline gene editing – deliberately changing the genes passed on to children at the embryo stage – research via the "maggot bots." BrightBorn chief Evie Cho (Jessalyn Wanlim) is so bent on curing her own ailments and creating "perfect" infants through this research that she wants the Leda line terminated altogether.

Manson explains what the maggot bot implanted into Sarah does to her. "It is trying, by a process of elimination, to determine why she is fertile. Whatever it is that has made Sarah immune [to the genetic illness] and fertile, that has made her the anomaly among the clones. It's flipping genomic switches on and off, trying to make her sick. [BrightBorn are] trying to flip switches to see if they hit the 'right' button. It's an entirely irresponsible, unethical form of scientific research."

Manson points out that creating life is a premise that underlies much classic science fiction. "I think there's a fundamental human hubris in trying to play God. That's a trope of a lot of great sci-fi. [Orphan Black] has that element. It's [also] got the banality of evil, because once you've done that, you have to administrate the whole thing," embodied by the scientists and their facilitators in the show.

"I always really liked that existential dilemma," Manson adds, "a little like the movie *Brazil*, or Franz Kafka, those kinds of existential stories."

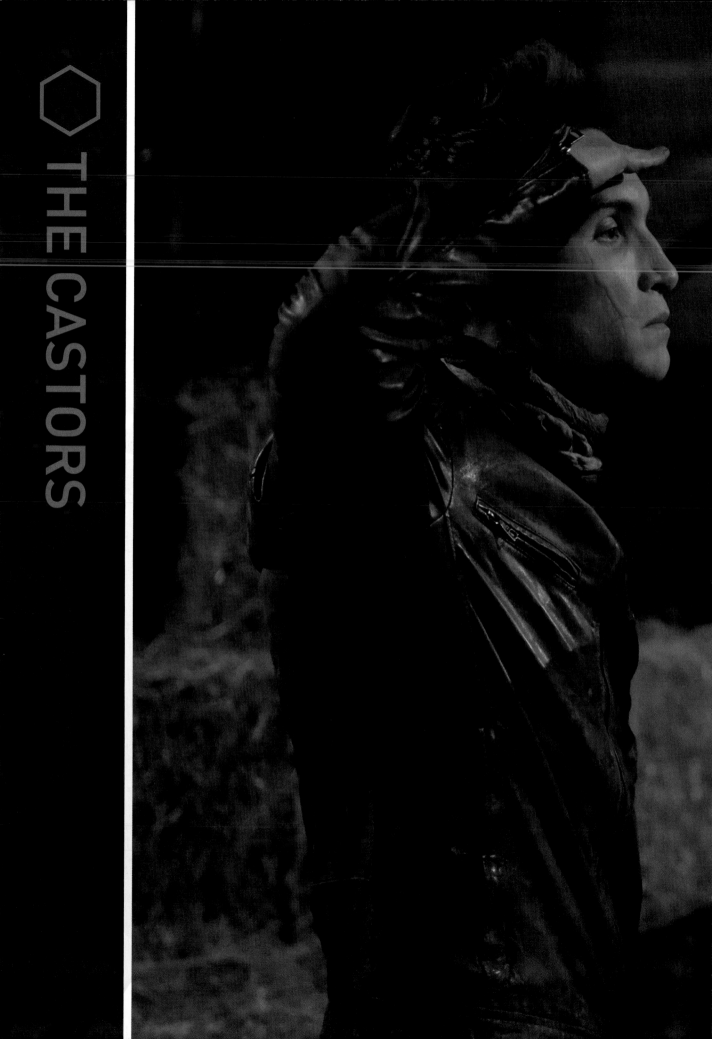

FACTS + FIGURES

Place of Birth: Unknown
Date of Birth: Unknown
Gender: Male
Hair Color: Brown
Eye Color: Hazel
Height: 5'10"
Portrayed by: Ari Millen
Appearances: 2.all except 2.07, 2.08; 3.all except 3.01, 3.07, 3.08

"*I always saw him as having two personas, the in-town persona, which was the muscle he was hired to be, and then the lost boy that he was back at the ranch.*"

When we first meet Mark Rollins, played by Ari Millen, he is the right-hand man of Prolethean leader Henrik Johanssen (Peter Outerbridge). Mark is a steely kidnapper and assassin, but he has growing feelings for Johanssen's daughter Gracie (Zoé de Grand'Maison) that finally lead him to run away with her. At the end of Season Two, we discover just how much Mark has given up – when we meet the male Castor clones, we realize Mark is one of them, and he's turned his back not only on Johanssen, but on his true assignment to spy on the Proletheans.

Jordan Gavaris says, "Ari's fantastic. He has this gravitas. There's something deep and mysterious about him as a person in life, and about his energy that he brings to all of his characters."

When Millen was first cast as Mark, he didn't know that Mark was a clone, because the creators didn't know it yet either. So would he have played Mark differently if he'd been told about Mark's origins? "I don't think I could not have. I'm very thankful that I didn't know."

That said, "My original take on him fed into the realization that he was part of Project Castor," Millen continues. "I always saw him as having two personas, the in-town persona, which was the muscle he was hired to be, and then the lost boy that he was back at the ranch under Johanssen, in the sense he probably didn't have a solid upbringing and was always looking for family, and he found it with Johanssen and the Proletheans. That fed into who he did turn out to be, but I played him as always looking for somewhere normal to belong."

Regarding Mark's feelings for Gracie, Millen opines, "Certainly being married, having a family, belonging was his ultimate goal. I think there was an instant attraction for Mark to Gracie."

"Certainly being married, having a family, belonging was his ultimate goal. I think there was an instant attraction for Mark to Gracie."

Lovers on the run Mark and cast-out
Prolethean Gracie [Zoé de Grand'Maison] [3.10]

Millen also enjoys working with the actress who plays Gracie. "Working with Zoé is always fantastic." Noting de Grand'Maison's resemblance to the main figure in the John William Waterhouse painting The Lady of Shalott, he adds, "It's very unique, this big, wild head of hair, but then such an innocent face, and what they have her doing in the plotlines is always so interesting."

One of Millen's favorite scenes is when Mark is shot in the leg, forcing him to accept help from Sarah with an impromptu surgery. "There was a lot of hitting the steps of doing this, cutting here, the blood coming out of the leg – there was all the technical side of it, but also, it was highly emotionally charged. This is the first

Mark and Paul (Dylan Bruce) agree to a temporary truce [2.06]

> "My original take on him fed into the realization that he was part of Project Castor. I played him as always looking for somewhere normal to belong."

time that Mark and Sarah are really connecting. Up until now, they've been enemies, or at least Mark's seen her as an enemy. All of a sudden, he has to put his trust in this woman, and he's just found out that they're related, too. There was a whole bunch going on there."

Technically, the surgery scene, with the puncturing of the leg and the gore, was all achieved with various physical effects. "They cut a hole in the couch and my leg's down underneath," Millen explains. "They've got a fake leg there that they got to cut into and then they sent the blood out."

It took a while to get the fake blood off. "That was another shower," Millen laughs. "You know what? The exact same scenes that were the toughest were the same ones that were the most enjoyable, just because I was really nervous about them leading into them, and then we did them, and then it was such a relief, and the pressure certainly helped me get to a place that I was very proud of."

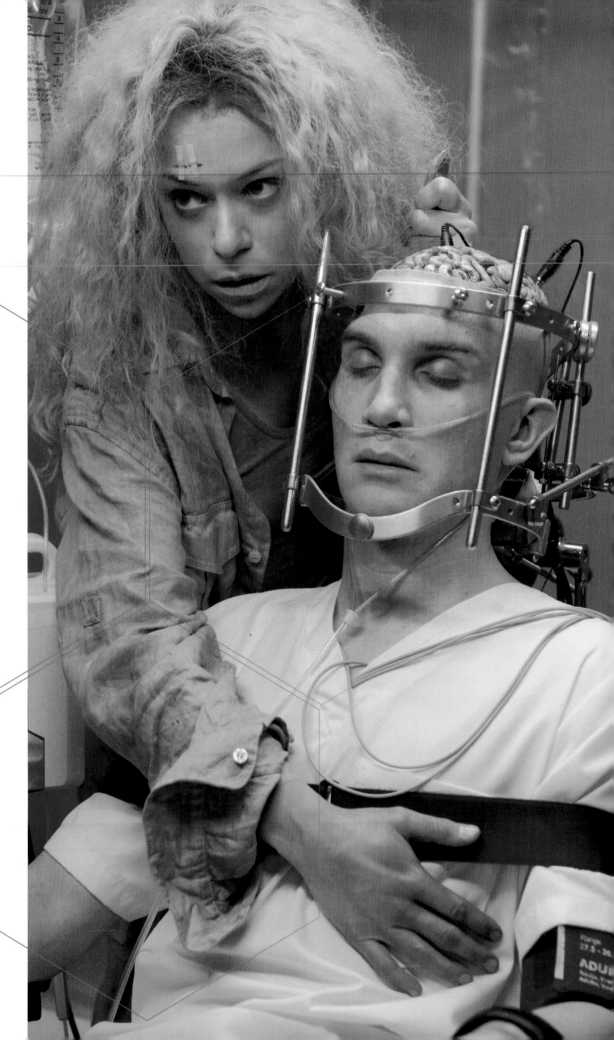

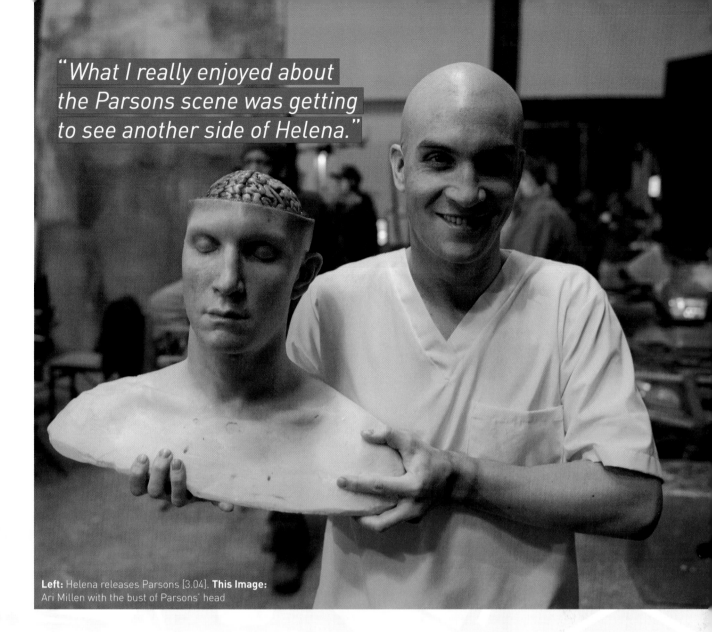

"*What I really enjoyed about the Parsons scene was getting to see another side of Helena.*"

Left: Helena releases Parsons [3.04]. **This Image:** Ari Millen with the bust of Parsons' head

Parsons is a Castor clone who Helena encounters while she is trying to escape from the military compound. Parsons is confined to a chair, his head immobilized by a metal apparatus. The top of his skull is gone, leaving his brain exposed for experiments Dr. Coady (Kyra Harper) is conducting in an attempt to cure the Castor disease. As angry as Helena is at Castor, she is driven to empathy by Parsons' condition. Wrongly thinking Sarah has betrayed her, Helena tells Parsons, "We were both abandoned by our families," before driving a scalpel into his brain and ending his agony.

"That scene, and the scene with Mark and Sarah doing the surgery," Ari Millen says, "I was dreading. The best scene of the season for me, the scene that I'm most proud of, was the surgery scene, but what I really enjoyed about the Parsons scene was getting to see another side of Helena. I was really happy with the work that we did for that scene."

Millen gives his perspective on how Parsons' exposed-brain effect was achieved. First, he says, a cast was taken of his head, front, top and back. "So they had this bust of my head, that on the top, they designed an exposed brain. That went back to the visual effects people as far as me sitting in this chair [on set, in character as Parsons] with the head apparatus on. I was in that chair for five hours. It was crazy. I didn't get out. And then when I finally did get out, they put the bust in and locked off [the camera, so that] they could use that brain as the visual and then they could fix it up, put blood on it and stuff in post [production]. So it was quite an undertaking and pretty cool."

RUDY

Rudy is a Castor military clone distinguishable by his attitude, hairstyle and scars, in particular his prominent facial scar. Makeup designer Stephen Lynch explains, "My initial idea was for his scar to be maybe three-quarters of the way around the eye, as if he almost lost it. Actually, Ari [Millen] and John [Fawcett] came up with the long, jagged scar, and so we did several designs and came up with that one. His back is covered in scarring [from] shrapnel and bullet wounds to suggest a backstory."

As for Rudy's faux-hawk haircut, Millen says, "He's kind of cock of the walk and a bit of a peacock, so I think that was how it manifested. I'm more of an introverted type of person, so getting to play someone like Rudy was a bit of an outlet for me. It's kind of fun to be wacky like that sometimes, and I really enjoyed it."

Rudy threatens practically everybody, including

Rudy snatches Kira [3.02]

little Kira (Skyler Wexler), Cosima's gentle lab colleague Scott (Josh Vokey) and even Scott's cat. Millen says, "My favorite Rudy scene might have been Kira, it might have been with Scott and the cat. Rudy got a lot of really great scenes."

Millen adds, "That cat was incredibly professional, I've got to say. It hit its lines every single take. It was forced to screech at a certain point, and it did every single take without being prompted. It was remarkable," he laughs. "It even threw in a couple of improv ones that I think they kept."

Millen cites Helena as his favorite Leda clone, in spite of the fact that, or perhaps because, she fatally wounds Rudy, then lays down and talks with him as he dies. "It was an inevitable death," Millen observes. "He was probably the least redeemable of all the new Castor clones, so he wasn't someone that could survive, but I certainly didn't want him to go. Though I was

"*He's kind of cock of the walk and a bit of a peacock... I'm more of an introverted type of person, so getting to play someone like Rudy was a bit of an outlet for me.*"

very happy that it was at Helena's hands. To a certain extent, they had that connection with each other, like no one else might, because they were most off the handle."

A lot of actors talk about experiencing a sense of grief when their characters die, but often that's tied to ending their work on a project. Though Rudy's death in "History Yet to Be Written" hasn't taken Millen off of *Orphan Black*, it was the end of playing a character who had appeared in nine previous episodes. "I think I didn't experience any of that until we were finished shooting it, because there was no time to slow down and reflect," says Millen of playing Rudy for the final time. "From conceptualizing to death was a whirlwind, and so I'm still processing it. I miss doing this with this guy, I miss doing that with that guy, but it's part of the job."

"*My favorite Rudy scene might have been Kira, it might have been with Scott and the cat. Rudy got a lot of really great scenes.*"

Top: Rudy dying next to Helena [3.10].
Above: Rudy threatens to hurt Scott's cat [3.08]. **This Image:** Rudy and Kira [3.02]

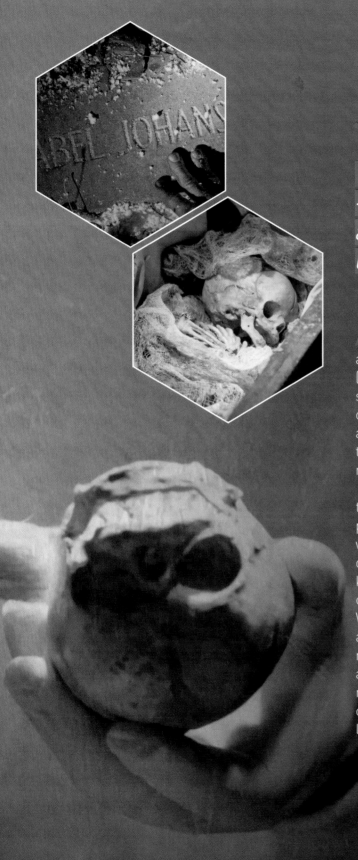

ABEL JOHANSSEN

> *"We're not just doing the casket – we're doing forty other things at once all the time. There are a lot of people involved."*

Abel Johanssen is a Castor clone developed by Henrik Johanssen (Peter Outerbridge), who used the original (stolen) Castor DNA and his own sperm and had his wife Bonnie (Kristin Booth) carry the embryo. Abel did not survive. The infant's remains are uncovered on the Johanssen ranch by Sarah and Mark, as the latter believes Abel's remains may hold the key to finding a cure for the Castor clones' neurological condition.

"The dead baby skeleton prosthetic was lent to us by another BBC America show," says production designer John Dondertman. "Then we made the little casket. My set designer draws up the box and details it, so the guys know what they're building and its scale. The carpenters build the box, the painters scenic it. We age it with layers of glaze and paint, hack away at it, splinter some of the wood out, and make it look like it had been in the ground for a while. That requires a lot of attention. We're not just doing the casket – we're doing forty other things at once all the time. There are a lot of people involved."

Top: Abel's headstone. **Above:** Abel's skeleton in its casket. **This Image:** Abel's skull is examined by Dr. Coady's team (3.04)

SETH

CHARACTER
PROFILE

Right: Seth questions Mrs. S in search of Ethan Duncan [3.01]. **Below Right:** Seth takes a neurocognitive analysis test [3.02]

"Seth I was just getting to know. I think I would have had the most fun of all with him had he survived... There was a bit of a goofball side of him that I liked to play with."

When we meet Seth, who is physically distinguished by the moustache he sports, he is already succumbing to the "glitching" brain deterioration that plagues the Castor clones. Seth becomes so ill that, while they're on a futile mission to get information from Sarah, his brother Rudy shoots him as an act of mercy.

"Seth I was just getting to know," says Ari Millen. "I think I would have had the most fun of all with him had he survived. Not only did he make me look like my grandfather, which was fun, but there was a bit of a goofball side of him that I liked to play with."

The disease afflicting the Castor clones has elements of encephalitis. "We had an initial conversation," Millen recalls. "[John and Graeme] always thought of it as mad cow disease for humans. To a certain extent, Rudy manifested it in a paralysis in his arm. For Seth, it started with eye twitches and then other paralysis. Because it was something attacking the brain, there really wasn't a right answer or a road map of, first this symptom, then that symptom, so I was free to play with that. But certainly with Seth, [in the scene before his death,] he was already far progressed. Paralysis was taking over, and [there were] blockages to the brain, where you can't find words or you [speak in] non sequiturs or nonsensical things that he was saying, so I just took what was in the script and added a little bit here, a little bit there."

As the actor who plays all the Castor clones, Millen admits that shooting Seth's death scene was difficult. "Yeah. I mean, there's a little bit of excitement, too. 'Hey, I get to kill myself.' But it was sad, because I really liked Seth and I didn't want him to go, but then *Orphan Black* creates such amazing scenarios and opportunities."

STYLES MILLER

CHARACTER PROFILE

" Miller was a strict badass.
He was a no-bullshit guy."

Styles Miller is only ever seen in the military compound and in his uniform. He is involved in waterboarding Helena and present during her neurological test. "Miller was a strict badass," says Ari Millen. "He was a no-bullshit guy, so that was interesting for me to play with that kind of personality, because normally, I'm never serious. I drive Sandra, my [real-life] fiancée, crazy, so breaking that mold for me was really interesting."

Hair designer Sandy Sokolowski worked to subtly differentiate the military Castor clones from one another. "That's three hairpieces on [Millen]. What we were going for is under the radar, military background mercenary types."

The Castor haircut, Sokolowski elaborates, is "Short and tight. We could try to do different things with the short hairstyle, which started off with Mark, who was the first [Castor clone]. You had that really short, tight hair. The whole first part was not a wig [at first]. Then it became a

wig eventually, but we were still stuck with the short hair."

For the Castor soldiers, costume designer Debra Hanson explains that John Fawcett didn't want uniforms that would define them as American or Canadian. "As soon as you do uniforms, because subconsciously, a lot of people know uniforms, every detail says something, so it's really hard. They are based on American uniforms, but they're derivative more than anything. We tried to neutralize them. The biggest thing was to make sure that they looked like they were in a warm climate, and that even though they might be associated with a particular military, the discipline might have been a little bit lax, so that certain ways of wearing the uniform, or when they would wear a T-shirt and not their jacket, would be not defined. And they were like Black Ops, where they weren't following any rules [regarding uniforms] that we are really aware of."

"*I see him as almost Susan Duncan's doll. She's molded him in the way that she wants, her ideal, or her twisted views.*"

Ira tests Rachel's robotic eye [4.03]

ra is the anomalous Castor clone. He was separated from the other Castor clones and placed with an upper middle class foster family by Susan Duncan (Rosemary Dunsmore) when he was four years old. Susan then met him again when he was attending Yale University, and the two became lovers. He has a warm, brotherly relationship with Charlotte (Cynthia Galant), the youngest of the Leda clones whom Susan took in after the death of Marian Bowles (Michelle Forbes). Ira doesn't mind much that Rachel is brought into their home, in "History Yet to Be Written," until he realizes that Susan and Rachel's ambitions take priority over curing his illness.

Millen says of Ira, "I think the goal was to make him as androgynous as possible. He grew up completely separate from the military Castors. He was taken away almost immediately by Susan, raised in a very cold, distant [environment], and then came back [as an adult] to live with Susan. I see him as almost Susan Duncan's doll. She's molded him in the way that she wants, her ideal, or her twisted views. Ira, because he was raised separately from Castor, and then another generation out from Leda, does not have any familial connections to Rachel or to anybody else. But he essentially knows what Rachel knows."

Ira's separation from his brothers allowed for a different Castor look. "He is very polished, very pristine, perhaps cosmetically altered, perhaps he's had his nose fixed," makeup designer Stephen Lynch relates. "I don't think he'd be averse to [using cosmetics], and I suspect he's had Botox as well, and peels."

How can someone be made to look like they've used Botox when they actually haven't done anything to their face? "Mostly with airbrushing," Lynch explains. "His makeup is ninety percent airbrush, which is really fun to do. I've been able to get some things through that airbrush that I didn't think one could. He is slightly opalescent, slightly unreal."

Clockwise from This Image: Ira shows Sarah BrightBorn files on germline editing carriers [4.09]. Ira and Rachel [4.07]. Ira calls for the helicopter to the island [4.10]

In Greek mythology, Castor is one of the twin sons of Leda; the other twin is Pollux. Though it can vary in different sources, generally Castor's father is said to be Leda's husband the king of Sparta, while Pollux is the child of chief god Zeus.

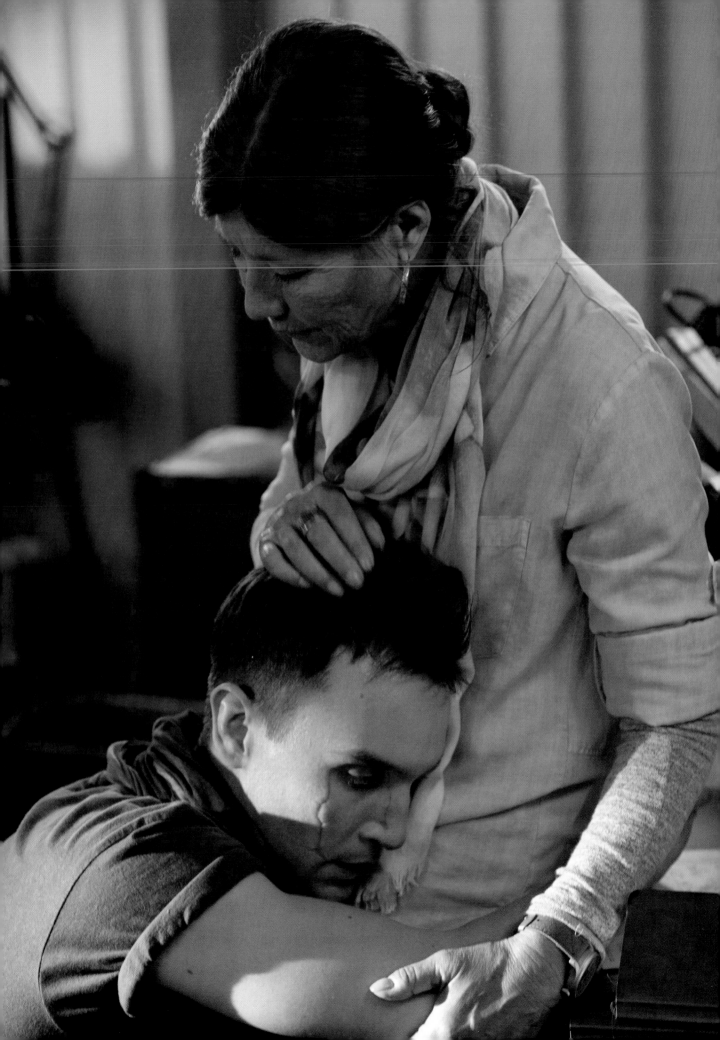

Opposite: Rudy seeks comfort from mother figure Virginia Coady [3.03]. **This Image:** Rudy taunts Helena while she's a captive of the Castor clones [3.03]

n *Orphan Black*, the Castor clones, all played by Ari Millen, are the product of Kendall Malone's male gene line. They have been genetically engineered to sexually transmit a disease that sterilizes women, so that they can decimate population growth in enemy nations. Unlike the female Leda clones, most of the Castor clones have a common upbringing in the military, under the command and supervision of Colonel – and Dr. – Virginia Coady (Kyra Harper). Though Coady is an officer willing to sacrifice the Castor clones on the battlefield or off for what she deems the greater good, the military Castors essentially regard her as their mother. Most of the Castor soldiers also have high regard for former compatriot Paul Dierden (Dylan Bruce).

"We really wanted to introduce male clones," says John Fawcett. "That was an important story element for us. But we had not settled on who it was going to be. There were many discussions about [which character] that could have been. There were also discussions about creating a new character that we would start seeding in towards the end of Season Two. Ultimately, we did even better, because we had a character that was seeded in right from the beginning of the season, and not just for the last two episodes."

That character turned out to be Millen's Mark Rollins, introduced as a loyal Prolethean. The Proletheans (and the viewers) have no idea that Mark's a spy. In fact, Fawcett relates, at the start, Mark "was a character that was going to be around as a bad guy causing problems for Sarah for the first six episodes, and then we were going to dispatch him. Then he had all these really weird, intimate, lovely little scenes with Zoé [de Grand'Maison, who plays Gracie Johanssen], and we were just like, 'We can't get rid of this guy, he's too interesting.'" The solution was to not only keep Mark, but cast Millen as the Castor clones.

Millen remembers getting the news. "Paul was supposed to kill Mark in ["To Hound Nature in Her Wanderings"], but every once in a while, I would have a chat with a writer or a producer, and they

Mark and Paul watching as Helena decimates a diner [2.06]

would say, 'We're really excited.' I was like, 'Okay, great, I'm going to get a fantastic death scene or something like that. Paul's going to destroy me and it's going to be brutal and gruesome like only *Orphan Black* can do.' And then the episode script came and I wasn't dead and so I started wondering what was going on. I was walking home one day and I got a phone call from Graeme, and he started off by thanking me for the season. I had no clue, because there was never any hint that they were going to do a male clone. He said, 'How

would you like to be the male clones?' My jaw dropped. I just said, 'Yeah, yeah, I think I can do that.' I sat down and had to catch my breath."

Just as Tatiana Maslany has Kathryn Alexandre as her clone double, Millen has Nick Abraham. "We had gone to theatre school together," Millen relates, "and when I found out that I was going to be a clone, I realized that they were going to need to cast a clone double. He was the first guy I thought of, selfishly, because he's my buddy, and I wanted him on the show to pick his brain. Also, I wanted someone that I knew, that I didn't have to break the ice with, we could just hit the ground running, because it was a whirlwind.

During pre-production, Nick and I went to an acting coach to help us figure these guys out. [The coach's] take on acting is figuring out who people are and their motivations. The physical was left to me, which I was happy to do. What I took away from that was developing each

Seth threatens Cal in Felix's stairwell [3.02]

"I was walking home one day and I got a phone call from Graeme... He said, 'How would you like to be the male clones?' My jaw dropped."

of their backstories and going back to those nuances and small differences and finding out what made them similar and what made them different. And from there, the collaborative process with hair and makeup and John and Graeme and then reading each episode."

Of playing multiple-clone scenes, Millen says, "The steep learning curve was having to remember that I had to be watching what Nick was doing and discussing in rehearsal, and making sure that the other clone in the scene was going to be doing what should be done, because once the master [shot] has been shot, that's how the scene has to play out. I couldn't concentrate on one character and go forward in the scene until we were shooting it. The rehearsal and the blocking, I had to be in two places at once, or three places at once. So that was a bit of a mind-blow."

While the Leda clones are all so different from one another, both physically and in their personalities, having most of the Castor clones be military makes it harder to distinguish them. But that, Graeme Manson explains, is because they introduced the Castor clones for a specific reason. "The concept of them being raised far more similar, aware of each other, aware that they're clones, putting them in a different psychological head space than the Leda clones, made them so fundamentally different, that when you realize that [Castor and Leda are] actually brother and sister, it makes that moment all the more shocking."

STRAND 2: THE OTHERS

FACTS ✚ FIGURES

Place of Birth: London, United Kingdom
Date of Birth: September 25,1989
Gender: Male
Hair Color: Brown
Eye Color: Brown
Height: 5'10"
Portrayed by: Jordan Gavaris
Appearances: 1.all; 2.all; 3.all; 4.all

"If you watch videos of Jagger and Bowie from the 1970s, there's a gender and sexual ambiguity about them that I loved for the character." – Jordan Gavaris

Felix Dawkins, played by Jordan Gavaris, is Sarah's foster brother. After getting over his shock at the clone situation, Felix helps the Leda women not just for Sarah's sake, but out of innate compassion.

"We liked Felix as Sarah's confidante," Graeme Manson says, "the chosen one true [platonic] love of her life, but also one true sibling of her life. We also have enjoyed straining that relationship over the seasons."

John Fawcett, who had previously directed Gavaris in an episode of *Unnatural History*, says, "The great thing about Jordan is that he works in a very similar way to Tatiana. They're very in-the-moment performers."

When Tatiana Maslany first did a Sarah/Felix scene with Gavaris in their audition, she says, "I felt like I'd known him my whole life. There was a bizarre, instant history between the two of us. He's one of my favorite people to play with, because he's so creative, emotional and funny."

Below: Felix demonstrates to Kira how to jump on a bed [2.10]. *Right:* Felix's biological half-sister Adele (Lauren Hammersley) with Felix [4.05]

"We liked Felix as Sarah's confidante, the chosen one true [platonic] love of her life, but also one true sibling of her life."

Gavaris says of Felix, "A lot of it was on the page." Though he auditioned using a variety of accents, including an American one. "How fey and vaudevillian he was, I think, was a direct result of the accent we settled on. There were some adjustments that had to be made that were specific to the [Thames] Estuary region he grew up in."

Fortunately, "We had John Nelles, our dialect coach [who also plays Male Nurse in the episode "By Means Which Have Never Yet Been Tried"], on set, working us through the accents. And now, it's relatively easy."

In terms of Felix's body language, Gavaris says that in real life, "I'm a lot more slouchy and lower to the ground. I used an animal exercise as a cat to find his physicality. His back is more rigid. By the end of the day, I'm pulling myself up, and arching my back backward a little bit, making sure I have less tension in my shoulders than I normally do, and it adds this lithe, loose, feminine physicality. And my lower back is always sore at the end of the day," he laughs.

"When we meet Felix, he's singular and

independent and not very concerned with what anybody else is going through," Gavaris observes. "He's a little irritated that Sarah's back in town, after being away for a year, and abandoned her daughter. He likes to keep things together, because if everyone is together and everyone is taken care of, no one will leave him. Then, as the sisters come together and the family bonds get stronger, it becomes obvious that he just likes to take care of people. I like taking care of people, too. Who you are will always inform your characters. You're exploring yourself when you're playing a character, so I think he's evolved and changed as much as I have. The writers never stop stretching him. As the episodes progressed, for me, it became less about performance and more about the experiential process of being this person."

Working with Maria Doyle Kennedy as Sarah and Felix's foster-mother Mrs. S, Gavaris says, "Feels like home. When we're working in S's house set, it's like we've just gone back to Mom and Dad's house."

In Season Four, Felix discovers that he has a biological half-sister, Adele, played by Lauren Hammersley. "Lauren is so bloody talented," Gavaris says. "She would try things on set; nothing precious about her process. It was extraordinary."

Clockwise from Left: Felix introduces Sarah to Adele [4.03]. Felix rocking fugitive chic [2.02]. A club kid (Jay Walker) and Felix dancing in Club Neolution [4.01]

"Who you are will always inform your characters. You're exploring yourself when you're playing a character, so I think [Felix]'s evolved and changed as much as I have."

Like his foster-sister, Felix is a survivor, which comes in handy as being an ally to Sarah and the other Leda clones can be dangerous. Shooting scenes involving physical violence can also be tough for the actors. When Paul, played by Dylan Bruce, violently forces Felix's hand onto a gun in order to get fingerprints to frame him, Felix is terrified. "Dylan is wonderful," Gavaris observes. "Physically, [Paul] is on top of [Felix]. I would never want to diminish what sexual assault actually feels like, but there was something sexually aggressive about it. I felt completely violated [as Felix]. So that scene was tough, but [episode director] Helen Shaver is a champ."

Bruce concurs, "That [scene] was pretty difficult, because on a Jordan/Dylan level, he's like a brother to me. And he really fought me there. He was so into his character, there was one take I think he actually spit at me."

Felix is a struggling artist and among his works seen on the show are portraits of Sarah and her "sestras" painted in his distinctive style. Various artists have created Felix's paintings during the show's run. In Season Three, Shelby Taylor did the artwork. Art director Jody Clement relates, "John Dondertman, the production designer, sat down with some reference of styles that he liked for Felix and together they worked on the basic design for each one of the pieces, and then Shelby painted them."

So does Felix's artistic talent reflect that of Gavaris? "Tat bought me a bunch of painting ingredients," Gavaris recalls. "I tried to make a painting, and it was the worst thing anyone had ever created. I physically burned the painting!"

However, Gavaris is interested in a lot of the issues raised in *Orphan Black*. "I think it's inevitable that you get interested in that stuff when you're playing in that world," Gavaris notes. "Like LGBTQ-related issues. I've always had a vested interest in science and medicine and biology. I like the recurring themes of nature versus nurture, corporate control. I like discussing those topics in a politicized and creative way on the show."

Felix as a character surprises Gavaris "routinely. There have been a lot of facets to his personality I wouldn't have expected, and the character has evolved over the course of the seasons. And I've evolved, too."

Left: One of Felix's self-portraits.
This Image: Felix, as is often the case, waiting for a sestra [2.04]

ARTHUR "ART" BELL

Opposite: Art talks to Helena (2.05). **This Image:** Detective Angela DeAngelis (Inga Cadranel), Lieutenant Gavin Hardcastle (Ron Lea) and Art at the station (1.09)

rt Bell, played by Kevin Hanchard, is a police detective who was Beth Childs' partner and, briefly, lover. Divorced and missing his kid, Art tries to help Sarah when he thinks she's Beth, and continues to help after he learns the truth, even if it means breaking the law.

Hanchard recalls his *Orphan Black* audition. "The main scene was where Art is interrogating Sarah, who he thinks is Beth, about the details of the Maggie Chen shooting and prepping her for her hearing. He knows that there's something wrong with her, but he's really holding her feet to the fire. It was a really wordy audition. I spent a lot of time working on it, so when we finally shot the scene, it was something I was familiar with, it was the heartbeat of what that relationship was."

Art's apartment reflects Hanchard's discussions with the writers. "John [Fawcett] and I had several casual conversations," Hanchard says. "We talked about the fact that I'm a huge football fan, about my kids and video games. I don't think we talked about fish, but I had an aquarium for years in my house. A lot of the things that we talked about manifested themselves in the set. It's a very smart use of space, which really speaks to who Art is."

Art is arguably *Orphan Black*'s most put-upon character. "No doubt," Hanchard laughs. "Art is used for his police connections. Everybody knows he's all in, based on his relationship with Beth. There was definitely a romantic feeling on his part. There's also that survivor guilt when your partner takes their life. When you feel you've let them down, you need to get to the bottom of it. He's not a guy who gets pushed around very much

> *"Art is used for his police connections. Everybody knows he's all in, based on his relationship with Beth."*

This Image: Art hunts the sniper [2.05]. **Inset Bleow Left and Right:** Art investigates dead clones Beth and Katja [1.08]

"Conversations are happening as a result of this show that weren't happening before, not only about cloning, but about human sexuality and love and the different forms of it."

by anybody, but I think that gnawing knot in the pit of his stomach is what allows him to do things he wouldn't otherwise do."

One of Hanchard's favorite scenes is "where Felix is drunk, and Art is trying to deal with that, and ultimately, they fell on top of each other on the couch. Jordan's a whole lot of fun to work with. One of the great things about working on the show is that there's a lot of improv. There's not a lot of improv that gets to happen with Art, but when you do get a scene like that, it's great to be able to play with it. And to work with someone as talented as Tatiana is great."

However, with Art and Paul being the two main men – and relationships – in Beth's life, Hanchard is sorry he didn't get more scenes with Dylan Bruce's Paul. "I'd have loved to flesh out what that rivalry was about," he explains, "how Art felt about Paul and how Paul felt about Art."

The reaction to *Orphan Black* has had an impact on Hanchard. "Conversations are happening as a result of this show that weren't happening before, not only about cloning, but about human sexuality and love and the different forms of it. A lot of the fan art and responses that we get have to do with people feeling like they finally see versions of themselves on TV. They finally have a storyline that speaks to them specifically. Girls talk about seeing positive female role models and heroes on television, and just being empowered. I'm a parent of a young daughter, and anything that helps empower her and makes her feel mighty is worth its weight in gold as far as I'm concerned."

Paul Dierden, played by Dylan Bruce, is Beth Childs' lover and monitor at the time of her death. He subsequently becomes Sarah's lover, and ultimately gives his life for her.

At the outset, "I knew he was Beth's boyfriend, he was a monitor, he fell in love with an impostor pretending to be Beth," Bruce says. "He did three tours of service in Iraq and Afghanistan as a soldier, in the intelligence field, and as a private contractor, so he was a badass. He killed Marines in a friendly fire accident in Afghanistan. I always thought that Paul would have PTSD."

Bruce's screen test for Paul opposite Tatiana Maslany was "probably one of the best auditions of my life. They're such powerful scenes, [and] it was really cool to play with Tatiana." As to why he was cast as Paul, Bruce has a theory. "When I was younger, I used to [hear] that I look like [Alias actor] Michael Vartan. John Fawcett and Graeme Manson were huge Alias fans. I [thought], maybe there's something in their heads saying, 'Cast this guy because he looks like Michael Vartan.'" He laughs. "I don't know if that's true."

Bruce is full of praise for the other Orphan Black cast members, and singles out two in particular. "I don't think anybody else can play [Felix] except Jordan Gavaris," he says. "Kristian [Bruun]'s so good, the character [of Donnie] just built and got bigger and bigger."

During his time on the show, it is revealed that Paul knew about the Leda and Castor clones from the outset. So, in Bruce's opinion, does Paul realize immediately that Sarah is not really Beth? "I think he thinks it's Beth," Bruce

"I knew [Paul] was Beth's boyfriend, he was a monitor, he fell in love with an impostor pretending to be Beth."

PAUL DIERDEN

Inset Left: Paul talks to Sarah [2.01]. **This Image:** Paul poses as Alison's lover with Sarah-as-Alison [1.06]

"Best material I've ever been given. Best cast I've ever been around. Tatiana is an amazing person, actress and spirit. It was like lightning in a bottle."

Opposite Inset Top: Paul in uniform [2.10].
Opposite Inset Bottom: Sarah with a
wounded Paul before he dies [3.06]. **This**
Image: Paul visits Helena while she's a
Castor prisoner [3.03]

replies. "The woman was so high on medication
and drinking and in such an unstable place that
to see her make a transition into a different
personality, almost, wasn't shocking to him."

Paul dies when, having been shot and stabbed,
he pulls the pin on a grenade in the hopes of
taking the Castor project out with him. "They
had twenty minutes with the stunt coordinator to
map out this fight," Bruce recalls of shooting the
scene. "The knife didn't have a blade on it – they
added the blade in post – so reacting to the knife
stabs while I had [Ari Millen] in the headlock was
a little awkward. When Dr. Coady shoots Paul,
nothing came out of the gun. They added the
gunpowder and smoke in post, too, then put two
bullet holes on me."

Bruce asked which side gets shot first so
he could react convincingly. "The on-set gun
handler said, 'It's like getting hit with a baseball
bat.' That's why you see my shoulders go left and

right, and then back."

By the end of that sequence, "It was 3 a.m.,
and prop blood gets hard. It had gone through
my pants and stuck to all the hairs on the side
of my leg and dried. I had to stand in the shower
with all my clothes on, with the wonderful on-set
costume guy, Peter Webster, spraying water
around where all the blood was on my leg, so
I could pry my pants off without ripping all the
hairs off of my leg," he recalls. "Then I got a
bottle of Scotch from Graeme Manson."

However, Paul's heroic death scene was not
the last scene Bruce shot. "It would have been
great to go out on that note, but I did one more
scene where I just get out of the jeep."

Summing up his *Orphan Black* experience,
Bruce says, "Best material I've ever been given.
Best cast I've ever been around. Tatiana is an
amazing person, actress and spirit. It was like
lightning in a bottle."

KIRA MANNING

CHARACTER PROFILE

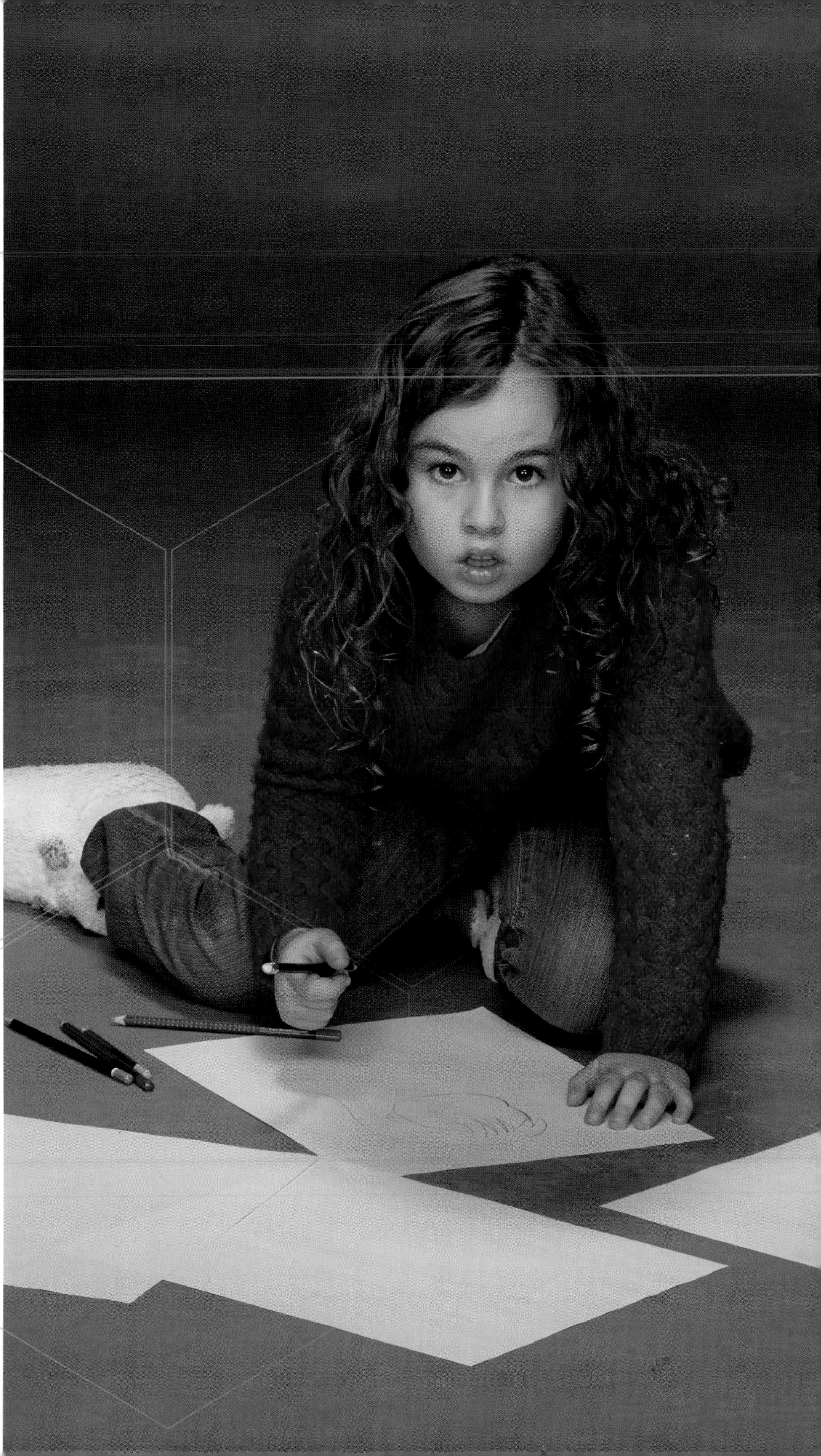

Virtually every action Sarah Manning takes is to protect her daughter Kira, played by Skyler Wexler. Kira is the only known naturally conceived child born to a clone (from Sarah's affair with Cal Morrison).

"I find it fun to play Sarah as a mother," Tatiana Maslany says, "because she's an unlikely candidate for the job. She desperately loves her child, but she's not necessarily equipped. She's got a lot of great instincts, but she also has instincts to run and be solo. That's how she's always been, so to have somebody who depends on her is a hard thing. But I really enjoy that dynamic, and Skyler is such an incredible actor, so it's a real treat for me."

Ari Millen echoes Maslany's admiration for Wexler's talent when he recalls shooting the scene where Castor clone Rudy manhandles Kira in "Transitory Sacrifices of Crisis." "Between takes, she'll be singing and joking around, and then, 'Oh, it's serious,' and, boom, into serious," Millen says. "There was never any fear after the first take."

Mrs. S is also a maternal figure in Kira's

"I find it fun to play Sarah as a mother, because she's an unlikely candidate for the job. She desperately loves her child, but she's not necessarily equipped. She's got a lot of great instincts, but she also has instincts to run and be solo."

life. Maria Doyle Kennedy opines that Mrs. S feels equally maternal toward Sarah and Felix, but, "She displays [her maternal feelings] differently, because she expects a different level of responsibility and reaction and motivation from Sarah and Felix than she does from Kira. Also, Kira hasn't developed any kind of teenaged relationship yet, so there haven't been any crazy standoffs with her."

Sometimes Kira has visions of her Mommy and "aunties," which she draws. Art director Jody Clement relates, "Sasha Kosovic is our art department apprentice, and any time we require some very specific scripted pieces of artwork, Sasha does those. That being said, Skyler, the actress, when you put crayons and paper in front of her on set, she gets right into it and will often draw, based on [the artwork] that Sasha has provided."

Is she psychic? "To me, it's a beautiful little

"That mystery is the most human thing about her. It's ineffable, and I don't know whether we'll ever put our finger on it. Why would you want to?"

mystery," says Graeme Manson. "That mystery is the most human thing about her. It's ineffable, and I don't know whether we'll ever put our finger on it. Why would you want to?"

While young actress Wexler is aging normally over *Orphan Black*'s five seasons, the events of the complete series are meant to be unfolding over the span of a few months, so keeping Kira from looking like she's growing too quickly is a production challenge. "It's sort of, 'Hey, fans, we're making a show, it took five years,'"

Manson notes with a laugh. "It gallops along at a pace where we're all going to have to suspend disbelief a little."

Costume designer Debra Hanson explains, "Some of it is tricking the eye, trying to find clothes that are really similar, but in a size that fits her now. She is growing, and the girlish clothes for somebody in her age group are not quite the same. So we've had to do an intense search. For some of that, we used the clothes that [she already had] and rebuilt them a little bit, to make them fit in the same way as clothes fit her when she was younger. She's a wonderful actress, so she's got that. We measure her all the time – we're like, 'How much taller is she? Let's put a boot on her that doesn't have a heel.'

"Everything she wears is practical," Hanson adds, "but Kira's soft, she's artistic. There's always something about her clothes that says that."

Top: Kira and Rudy [3.02]. **Left:** Kira in bed with her beloved sock monkey just before it burns with the abandoned cabin [4.01].
Below: Kira's drawing of her "aunties"

AUNTIE ALISON   AUNTIE HELENA   AUNTIE COSIMA

Donnie Hendrix, played by Kristian Bruun, is the loving husband of Alison Hendrix, shocked but not alienated when he discovers Alison is a clone. He also supports Alison's schemes, whether she's running for the school board or becoming a drug dealer.

"Kristian Bruun is a remarkably good and very funny actor," says Graeme Manson. In fact, an improvised moment of comedy in his audition made it into the show. "The glue-gun torture scene! I didn't have a ton of time to prep it, so it was all straight from the gut. I improvised a little," Bruun recalls. "The writers, my first day on set, were telling me how much they loved this stupid thing I did in the audition, where, in between my lines, I was trying to blow out the hot glue on my chest with my breath."

Jordan Gavaris echoes Manson's sentiments. "Kristian is incredible to work with. He has an incomparable intellect, especially when it comes to comedy."

Not much was known about Donnie by either Bruun or the writers at the beginning. "He was just a schmucky husband from the suburbs," Bruun observes. "That's all they could really tell me. I didn't know if he was a bad guy or a good guy. I didn't find out that Donnie was a monitor until I'd read the last script for Season One. I think Donnie has grown in John and Graeme's minds, and also in my mind, and in the fans' minds."

"Kristian's amazing," Tatiana Maslany says of her on-screen husband. "He's one of my favorite people to play with; he's so open and fun. He really cares

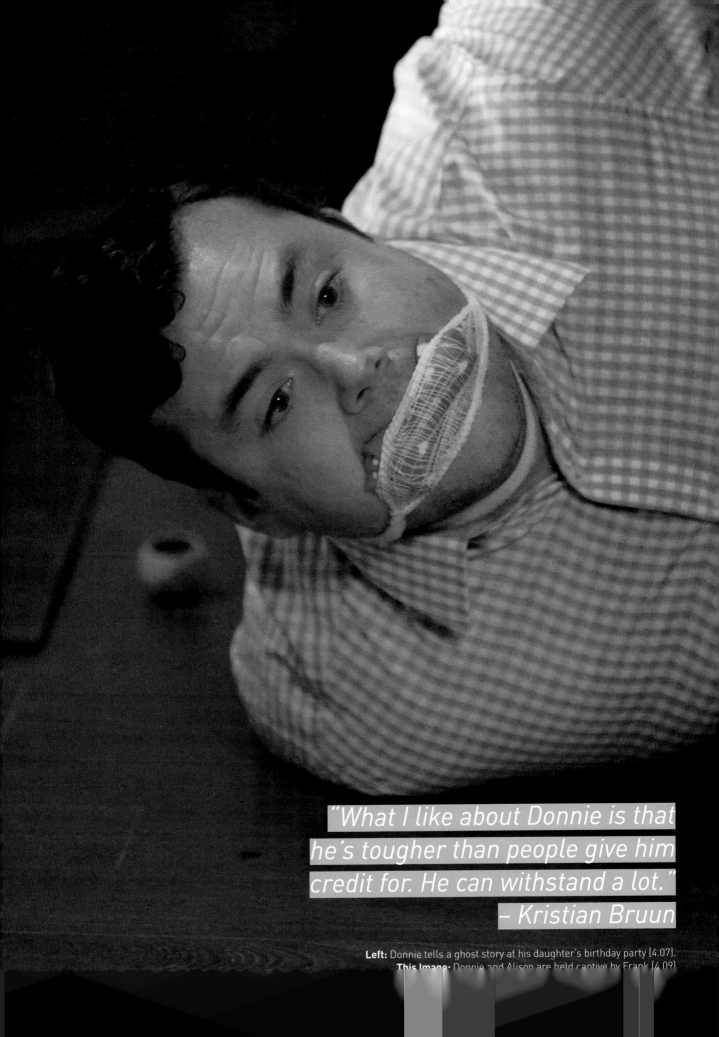

"What I like about Donnie is that he's tougher than people give him credit for. He can withstand a lot."
– Kristian Bruun

Left: Donnie tells a ghost story at his daughter's birthday party [4.07].
This Image: Donnie and Alison are held captive by Frank [4.09].

about Donnie, [who has] so many complexities to him. I think that's a real testament to Kristian. He doesn't keep Donnie in one place, and that's why people can't stop watching him."

Bruun greatly enjoys the scenes of Donnie as a father to the Hendrix children. "He loves being a dad," Bruun confirms. "I love working with Millie [Davis as Gemma] and Drew [Davis as Oscar]. They're brother and sister in real life, and so talented and so funny. Never in a bad mood."

When Donnie agrees to be part of an intervention for Alison, then calls a halt to it, in "Unconscious Selection," Bruun feels it's a turning point in the Hendrixes' marriage. "He realizes that these people are not helping her in the way that she needs, and he decides to step up and be a much better partner."

" [Donnie has] so many complexities to him. I think that's a real testament to Kristian. He doesn't keep Donnie in one place..."

Bruun also identifies another key Alison/Donnie moment as "The big confession between Donnie and Alison, and them burying Dr. Leekie's body and cementing his body into the ground, also [cementing] their relationship, consummating on top of the freezer that used to have dead Leekie."

Some of Bruun's favorite scenes are "between

Clockwise from Below: Donnie finds out about the clones [2.07]. Felix and Donnie pose as a couple [4.04]. The Hendrix family, Oscar (Drew Davis), Gemma (Millie Davis), Donnie and Alison, at Aynsley's funeral [2.02]

Alison and Donnie that get deeply personal in terms of their relationship. The comedy between Tat and I is easier, because we love joking around, and we know that for the most part our days on set [together] are full of energy and laughter, and a mood break for the crew and the cast, but also for the show, in terms of all the heightened drama. But it's the dramatic stuff I'm so glad they've given me.

"A lot of TV shows will pigeonhole you into one type of character and keep you there," Bruun observes. "[Orphan Black's writers] really have let Donnie grow quite a lot. I love finding a raw, dramatic edge to him when he needs it. And Tat is the perfect partner to work on that stuff, because she's so giving and authentic, always there for you."

Above: Donnie meets a threatening Neolutionist (Noah Danby) in prison [4.08].
This Image: Alison watches as Donnie lays down the law for Vic (Michael Mando) [2.09]

FACTS ⊕ FIGURES

Place of Birth: Dublin, Ireland
Date of Birth: September 22, 1965
Gender: Female
Hair Color: Brown
Eye Color: Blue
Height: 5′6″
Portrayed by: Maria Doyle Kennedy
Appearances: 1.all except 1.06; 2.all except 2.01, 2.03, 2.05; 3.all except 3.03, 3.04; 4.all except 4.01, 4.09

"It was clear to me from the beginning that she was going to be an interesting individual. She wasn't clearly all good or all bad."
– Maria Doyle Kennedy

Siobhan Sadler, aka Mrs. S, or just S, is played by Maria Doyle Kennedy. Mrs. S is the adoptive mother of Sarah Manning and Felix Dawkins (Jordan Gavaris). She's also the biological daughter of Kendall Malone (Alison Steadman), who is the original source of genetic material for the Leda and Castor lines. This means Mrs. S is half-sister to all of the clones.

Although few call her by her first name, Doyle Kennedy says, "I think of her as Siobhan. Mrs. S I think is the place of least vulnerability for her. Sarah says now, occasionally, 'Mum' or 'Siobhan,' but she'll still go back to 'S,' because it defined the relationship."

Doyle Kennedy was immediately drawn to Mrs. S. "She had elements of different types of behavior and motivations and contradictions, like real people," she says. "Then Graeme [Manson] told me the blueprint in his mind for Mrs. S was Patti Smith. So that was a done deal for me."

Additionally, "She was described as having been a radical or an activist. We don't get into really seeing how badass she can be until it comes to Season Two. That wasn't spelled out in Season One, but the words 'activist' and 'radical' mean something to me, and I had the feeling they meant something to Graeme as well, so I did feel that she was capable of fairly serious behavior in the pursuit of what she believed in. It seemed to me that she has a really strong moral code."

Costume designer Debra Hanson observes, "In the first season, S was quite soft, and often wore beautiful shawls and clothes that draped on her. In the second season, she started to be tougher and more physical, so we [gave her] slimmer silhouettes."

"My struggle is to keep Mrs. S from ever looking too glamorous, because [Doyle Kennedy] is beautiful," makeup designer Stephen Lynch says

Opposite: S at Ethan Duncan's house [2.06]. **This Image:** The divine Mrs. S sings, accompanied by Kieran (played by Doyle Kennedy's husband, Kieran Kennedy) on guitar [3.09]

"She was described as having been a radical or an activist... so I did feel that she was capable of fairly serious behavior in the pursuit of what she believed in. It seemed to me that she has a really strong moral code."

Clockwise from Above Felix and Mrs. S in the hospital waiting room [1.09]. Carlton (Roger Cross) and Siobhan [2.04]. Dr. Van Lier can't leave Mrs. S's side [4.10]. Mrs. S makes a deal for Sarah and Kira with Paul [2.10]

"I'd love to take her into that realm, but it wouldn't be right. She's an old punk and anarchist, and I want to keep her true to her roots."

In "Governed by Sound Reason and True Religion," Mrs. S turns to old comrades Barry (Rob deLeeuw) and Brenda (Nora McLellan), who she then kills when they betray her. "These were the people who shared the same ideals as her," Doyle Kennedy explains. "Brenda says she's tired of doing all this work and not having any money. Apart from placing them in danger, S is devastated by the loss of the ideal, the loss of the shared idea of cause. It's fundamentally destabilizing."

Mrs. S has many physical confrontations. "Fight scenes are always difficult [to shoot]," Doyle Kennedy notes, "because things become heightened in the moment, and I'm always terrified that I'll hurt somebody. I'm a strong woman," she laughs, "and I imagine I could pack quite a punch, should I let go. You worry

> "I think of her as Siobhan. Mrs. S I think is the place of least vulnerability for her. Sarah says now, occasionally, 'Mum' or 'Siobhan,' but she'll still go back to 'S,' because it defined the relationship."

less about getting hurt yourself, because your adrenaline is up. We have a really good stunt advisor, who will show us how to deliver things that look like absolutely fatal blows, and how to accept them as well."

There have also been "quite a few" scenes that have been emotionally difficult. "After I traded Helena and Ari Millen as Rudy beat me up, that's S at her most vulnerable," Doyle Kennedy says.

"It's probably the first time that she feels that she really screwed up. She was doing it for the right reasons, but it turned out not to be good for anybody. It was hard to think you've just betrayed your daughter and her sisters.

"The other really sad one was Alison Steadman playing Kendall, telling me that she was going to die, this mother that I couldn't stand, that I've reconnected with," Doyle Kennedy continues. "Both Alison and I cried and cried. I have such huge admiration for her, I've been a fan of hers for years."

The most fun scenes to shoot, for Doyle Kennedy, are "anything with Tatiana and Jordan and I. Sometimes we do a bit of improv, sometimes we slag each other or have fun or trade music that someone has found, but it's always great, because we spark off each other. Also, I've known James Frain [who plays Ferdinand] for a long time. We've acted together before [in the 1995 film *Nothing Personal* and in

the series *The Tudors*], so we have a lot of fun when we get scenes together."

In "Insolvent Phantom of Tomorrow" Mrs. S sings in a pub. In real life, Doyle Kennedy reveals, "I sing probably more than I act. I run my own record label with my husband, Kieran Kennedy, so that's a huge part of my life. I did a show in Toronto that Graeme and John came to. They approached me, and they wanted me to do a song [in *Orphan Black*]. It was very sweet of them. They wanted to use one of Kieran and my songs. The song is called 'Stuck,' and it's on the album *Mutter*."

The best thing about working on *Orphan Black*, for Doyle Kennedy, "is being part of a show that clearly loves women." She adds, "There are a lot of good things. I'm really interested in the idea of identity and how we form it, and nature versus nurture, and how different environments impact different genes. I think you can't really be human without being interested in those things."

VICTOR "VIC" SCHMIDT

CHARACTER PROFILE

"He was in rehab, so perhaps they were giving him lessons on how to be present and compassionate and kind. He really tried, and it didn't work."

Vic Schmidt, played by Michael Mando, is Sarah Manning's ex-boyfriend. A drug dealer and abusive yet needy, Vic is arguably the Wile E. Coyote of *Orphan Black*. Not as tough as he imagines, Vic tries to bully and blackmail Sarah, then goes to rehab in order to befriend and betray Alison, but all his schemes backfire, often violently. He's last seen, along with Detective Angela DeAngelis (Inga Cadranel), confused and being warned to stay away from Alison and her sisters by Donnie (Kristian Bruun) in "Things Which Have Never Yet Been Done."

Makeup designer Stephen Lynch observes, "[Mando is] very handsome. The challenge we had was that we needed to keep him really looking close to the street. Who knows where he's living? Eventually, he's selling stolen meat out of the back of a truck. So [he had to] look unhealthy and beat up and not manicured. I had to take him down, [give him] a general air of poor health, things breaking down, perhaps, old tattoos and discoloration around his eyes."

"Vic changed from Season One [in Season Two]," costume designer Debra Hanson relates, "going away from being the gangster tough guy and trying to find himself through mindfulness and becoming softer. The tight jeans were gone, there was a looser feeling to him. We had a mala for him, a Buddha piece of jewelry. Sometimes he'd wear it around his wrist, sometimes he'd wear it around his neck, because we felt that he was trying to meditate and settle his mind and become a happier person. He was in rehab, so perhaps they were giving him lessons on how to be present and compassionate and kind." She laughs. "He really tried, and it didn't work."

Vic could have been very different. Ari Millen, who plays the Castor clones, reveals, "I originally auditioned for Vic. Then Mark came up in the second season and I'm very thankful they held out for me."

"I really liked Michael Mando as Vic-the-dick," Graeme Manson concludes. "He sure got beaten into submission."

ALDOUS LEEKIE

CHARACTER PROFILE

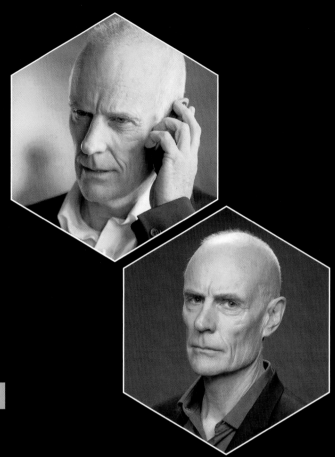

"He's in love with his own genius, and convinced that his genius is right for the world."

Dr. Aldous Leekie, played by Matt Frewer, seems to be in control of Neolution and the Dyad Institute when we first meet him. Shows what we know.

Costume designer Debra Hanson says, "He's in love with his own genius, and convinced that his genius is right for the world. So there's the whole cream and white thing happening."

Leekie's office décor likewise makes a statement, adds art director Jody Clement, who designed that set. "That was one of the most beautiful office spaces that I had the luxury to work on. We used Carrara marble tiles for the floor. The glass panels gave beautiful reflections when they were shooting through them. The tones of wood and leather couches really spoke to who Dr. Leekie was."

John Fawcett, who first worked with Frewer when he directed an episode of the miniseries *Taken*,

has a tale of the actor's prankish nature. "[*Taken*] was probably my biggest job to date. I had a scene with Frewer, first thing up on my first day. Matt had a paper bag on his head that had a sad face drawn on it. The producer said, 'Matt's wearing the bag this morning, so just go block the scene, don't mention the bag, and hopefully he'll take it off before we roll. He's a little bit of a strange one.'" Fawcett tried to block the scene around his bag-headed star before the crew burst out laughing and he realized it was a practical joke.

Fawcett and Frewer have worked together a number of times since, but on *Orphan Black*, the director says, "When Matt walked on set his first day, the entire crew was wearing paper bags. He couldn't figure it out at first. Then he realized that I was playing a joke on him, and what it was from. I got him back, ten years later."

"In the beginning, we weren't necessarily setting out to make a love story. It was really something that we found along the way."

A lot of fans have become extremely invested in "Cophine," the term coined for the romance between Cosima and Dr. Delphine Cormier, a Frenchwoman played by Quebec native Evelyne Brochu. Delphine starts out as one of Leekie's disciples and agrees to be Cosima's lab partner and monitor (Cosima suspects the latter when they first meet). Then Delphine falls for the already smitten Cosima.

"In the beginning," John Fawcett reflects,

"we weren't necessarily setting out to make a love story. It was really something that we found along the way. As we start to see fans and how they respond to different characters and relationships, you go, 'Oh, that's obviously working.' So you start to work that a little bit more and form it and it did take on this slightly bigger, epic love-story feel, which is great."

Though Fawcett adds, "I don't like to make big creative decisions based on what the fans

Below: Delphine Cormier at Dyad [2.01]. **Top Right:** Mentor Dr. Leekie (Matt Frewer) with Delphine and potential new recruit Cosima [2.01]. **Bottom Right:** Cosima's vision of Delphine [2.10].

want, because if we did that, I think Cosima would just be in bed with Delphine the whole time, doing science!"

"Delphine's classic," says costume designer Debra Hanson of the character's stylish looks. "She's very European, and very soft – soft blouses and not a lot of patterns. She has jackets, some tailored, and she's working for a big corporation. At the same time, there's a certain kind of romance to her, which is why I think she's so appealing to Cosima. And then we don't know which way she's going to go. She becomes tougher, and makes more money, and there's always a mystery: Does that appeal to her or not? Is she going to be consumed by Dyad and power? She's not sleek like Rachel, but she takes Rachel's job, so suddenly, there's a little bit

"There's a romance to her... [Then] she becomes tougher, and makes more money, and there's always a mystery... Is she going to be consumed by Dyad and power?"

of a sharper line, a little bit less of the romance in her, more formal, more money spent on herself, on her presentation. So that reflects in her wardrobe."

Like Rachel, Delphine tends towards blacks and creams in her wardrobe choices. "That's because she's working for Dyad," Hanson explains.

Clockwise from Left: Delphine tending to the grievously ill Cosima [4.10]. L'amour de Cophine [1.09]. Topside assassin Ferdinand Chevalier with Delphine [3.01]

"Everybody at Dyad is in blacks and creams, but hers are much softer than anybody else's."

"Delphine's awesome," says hair designer Sandy Sokolowski. "Her hair is naturally curly, so we wanted to keep it like that. As she got to be higher up in the food chain, she was more put together and we decided to round-brush it out and blow-dry it up."

Delphine's makeup also reflects her character, makeup designer Stephen Lynch explains. "Look at that face! She's so beautiful and such a favorite. I designed a look for her," Lynch says, "and actually Kristin [Wayne], my assistant, does her beautiful makeup. I think she's proud, I think she knows what she has and how to present it."

It appears that Delphine has been murdered at the end of Season Three, but viewers – and

Cosima – learn that she's alive toward the end of Season Four. Graeme Manson explains, "It's a show that demands drama and high stakes and missing people. You're faced with story choices of, what do we put in jeopardy that we've so painstakingly built up to be a fan favorite? We chose to do something dramatic with Delphine, but it was always in our back pocket, especially for myself, that Delphine would loop back into the story. So we worked really hard through the season to thread in lightly the concept that Delphine may not have actually died, always hoping that, toward the end of the season, we'd be able to bring the actor back and allow the Delphine/Cosima story to continue. We did it for the fans, and because it makes for a really good romantic story."

SCOTT SMITH

"[Like Scott,] John [Fawcett] is the huge comic book geek of the gang, and the tabletop board games fanatic."

Scott Smith, played by Josh Vokey, was a classmate of Cosima's at the University of Minnesota. Though at first unaware of exactly what he's looking into, Scott is a fellow scientist and helps Cosima with her clone research. Eventually, he ends up as her assistant at Dyad.

Part of Scott's story function is to demonstrate Cosima's gift for friendship. Costume designer Debra Hanson observes, "Even when Scott had his friend [in the lab], and she discovered they were playing a game, she was right in there. She's open somehow."

Scott's first loyalty is to Cosima over his employment at Dyad. So when Cosima leaves the company, Scott goes with her – along with his best friend, security guard Hellwizard (Calwyn Shurgold) – and they move the laboratory with all their research. Graeme Manson recalls, "We started talking about the [new] lab being under a comic book shop, which John [Fawcett] really loved and wanted to shoot."

Scott is passionate about the civilization-building board game Agricola, reflecting one of Fawcett's interests. "John is the huge comic book geek of the gang," Manson explains, "and the tabletop board games fanatic."

This Image: Scott (Josh Vokey) studies Rachel's paintings at Dyad [3.06].
Left: Cosima, Sarah and Scott in the lab under the comic book shop [4.03]

SUSAN DUNCAN

"Susan Duncan is not just evil. She's very rich in her ethics, in her science... She truly believes in her heart that she's trying to improve the human race and the human lot on the planet."

Professor Susan Duncan, played by Rosemary Dunsmore, developed the Leda clone line alongside her husband Ethan (Andrew Gillies). Susan and Ethan were the adoptive parents of Rachel Duncan and made her aware of her clone identity from a very young age. When there was a fire at the lab, Susan let everyone, including Rachel and Ethan, believe she was dead. Now Susan is the legal guardian of young Leda clone Charlotte (Cynthia Galant) and mentor/lover to Castor clone Ira. By the end of Season Four, we learn that Susan is in league with still-living Victorian-era Neolutionist P.T. Westmoreland.

"Susan Duncan is not just evil. She's very rich in her ethics, in her science," Graeme Manson says. "She's thought long and hard about what she's doing, and yes, she may be a eugenicist, but she truly believes in her heart that she's trying to improve the human race and the human lot on the planet."

THE DYAD INSTITUTE

The Dyad Institute is part of a larger multinational corporation, Dyad Corp., which oversees both the Leda and Castor projects. The corporation also encompasses BrightBorn, which was overseen by the murderously ruthless Evie Cho (Jessalyn Wanlim), who favored self-serving genetic research over the clone program. The Institute has been through a variety of chiefs during *Orphan Black*'s present-day timeline, including Aldous Leekie (Matt Frewer), Rachel Duncan and Delphine Cormier (Evelyne Brochu). Dyad publicly promotes the human enhancement philosophy of Neolution, and secretly performs experiments that include human cloning.

Costume designer Debra Hanson recalls that Dyad gave the production departments the opportunity to innovate. "John [Fawcett] said, 'I'm sick of seeing the same old medical things.' So we made these clear plastic [biohazard] suits, where you could see the [conventional garb] underneath. We actually had medical people call us and ask us where they could get them. We had to explain, 'No, no, they're not real bio-suits, they're just some made-up pieces of vinyl tablecloths that we made.' So that was fun."

This Image: Paul at the Dyad Institute [2.01]. **Opposite:** Neolutionist Trina (Allie MacDonald) [4.01]

At the outset of *Orphan Black*, Aldous Leekie (Matt Frewer) is the foremost proponent of Neolution. We learn later that Neolution was actually founded by still-living nineteenth-century scientist P.T. Westmoreland. Neolution promotes "self-directed evolution" and has gained a group of followers who like to hang out in a club called – of course – Neolution, where members have augmented eyes, ears and the like. Club Neolution proprietor Olivier Duval (David Richmond-Peck) has his own tail, though it is not a true vestigial tail, but was surgically attached.

Graeme Manson says that, while they do evil, both the Neolutionists and the Protheans have good arguments for their belief systems. "Just don't ask me to make them," he laughs. "Part of the fun of the show is that it is a mash-up, and we do try to do that with all of our characters as well. It's hard to find a villain in *Orphan Black* that doesn't have a part of them that you sympathize with at some point."

Proletheans, including (left to right) Bonnie (Kristin Booth), Gracie, Henrik (Peter Outerbridge), and Mark, pray for Helena (2.03)

The Proletheans are a religious group with a worldwide reach and an anti-clone agenda. They are responsible for brainwashing Helena into becoming an assassin. The branch the sestras come into contact with lives on a farm, under the leadership of Henrik Johanssen (Peter Outerbridge) and his wife Bonnie (Kristin Booth). Kathryn Alexandre plays the Prolethean Alexis; because only one Leda clone was on screen at a time with Alexis, it meant Alexandre wasn't needed to double Tatiana Maslany and could therefore be onscreen herself.

Although the Proletheans call the clones "abominations," Johanssen – previously part of the original team of scientists that created the Leda and Castor clones – is obsessed with impregnating Helena. Writer/producer Russ Cochrane says, "We knew Helena was going to break out of the Prolethean compound, which was fun to figure out. [John Fawcett] said, 'There's a barn on the location and I want her to run through the barn, and it's crazy what's in there.' I said, 'What's in there?' He said, 'I don't know. Maybe they're making a bomb.' He wanted something that was incongruous with the pastoral landscape. I said, 'Oh, you mean, she runs in and it's a lab.' And he said, 'Yes! What are they doing?' I said, 'I don't know yet.' I came in the next day and basically pitched the episode ["Governed As It Were By Chance"], kind of as it ended up playing. Helena runs through the barn when she escapes and sees the lab, which triggers a flashback, then later she rescues Sarah from Daniel. When she comes in, she's terrifying to Sarah, who thought she was dead, but then Helena crumples at her feet and says, 'Sarah, they took something from me.' It's in that moment that we find out when we come back to the Proletheans that they had extracted Helena's eggs and were doing artificial insemination. When I pitched that, everybody in the room went, 'Ooh! They took her eggs. They're going to get her pregnant.'"

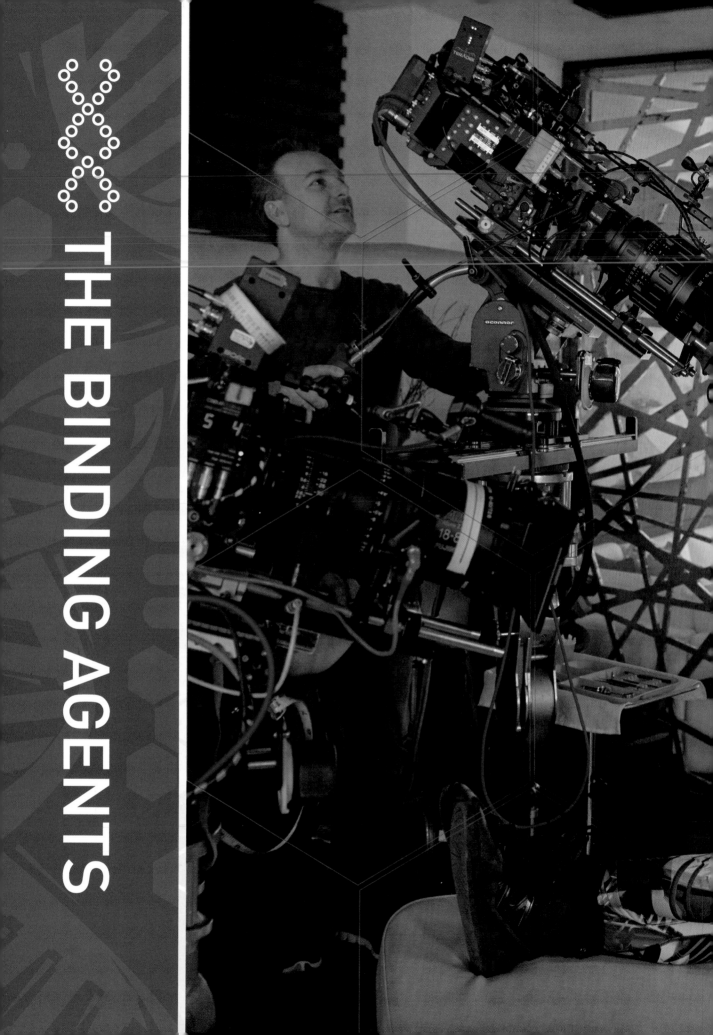

THE BINDING AGENTS

Costume designer Debra Hanson, who is in charge of her own department, says, "We [wardrobe, hair, makeup] all work together." Whenever a new Leda clone is going to be introduced, "Hair and makeup and I will meet with Tatiana and the producers and the creators, and we'll have a big meeting, and talk about her. We all share thoughts and images before we go at it.

"Once I have a costume, then I show it to everybody and people go, 'Yeah, that's great,' or [they don't], so that we're all hand in hand together."

The costumes are usually purchased rather than manufactured. "We make specialty things," Hanson explains. "The wedding dress for Helena, for instance, we made about six or seven of those, because of the different stages of breakdown that it goes through. Every season, I make some pieces, but I would say that the vast majority of it is bought.

"I'm proudest that the actors feel that the character is wearing their own clothes," Hanson replies when asked what she likes best about her job. "I don't think I have anybody who is unhappy, thinking that they are dressed in the wrong style or the wrong piece. I think actors, when they go to set, are comfortable that they're wearing the right skin."

Similarly, makeup designer Stephen Lynch says he's proudest of "making an actor's job easier. It is my reward if someone says, 'Thanks, I look in the mirror and I see this person, I know who she is.' [That's] the highest compliment I could receive. Not a beautiful makeup, not a startling makeup, not a stunning makeup, but something from their inside that is now tangible and visible. It's the best compliment I could ever receive when an actor says, 'I know who I am now and I didn't when I sat down in the [makeup] chair.'"

Hair designer Sandy Sokolowski describes *Orphan Black*'s overall hair aesthetic as "always real. Every character has a backstory in my mind, a time before that character hit the screen. In the case of Helena, she would have escaped, she would have had this bad color job that was growing out from the roots, and she wouldn't spend a lot of time on it."

The wig changes on Leda clones take about thirty minutes each and Leda clone double

Previous Spread: Wanlim, Alexandre, Maslany, and crew members [4.06]
Opposite: Some of Felix's artworks – Sarah, Alison, Cosima.
Top: Millen examining a Mark wig. **Above:** Millen back to back with Castor clone acting double Nick Abraham

Kathryn Alexandre has her own set of wigs. There are backup wigs, but only one "hero" wig per character. This is because the cost of a wig can be anywhere from five thousand to eight thousand dollars. They cannot be quickly replaced, either. "It takes me about three weeks to make a wig," Sokolowski explains.

"When you see it on the screen, when you believe it to be true, there's a lot of work that goes into everything to make it that way," says Sokolowski of working on a show as complex as *Orphan Black*.

The number of soundstages and standing sets varies on *Orphan Black* from season to season. For instance, on Season Four, producer Claire Welland reports, there were two stages. "It's about thirty-five thousand square feet, together with the two stages." There were also ten standing sets, which is more than is usual for a television series. "We have all our sets,

> "I'm proudest that the actors feel that the character is wearing their own clothes... I think actors, when they go to set, are comfortable that they're wearing the right skin."

Clockwise from Above: Season One front door of Felix's loft. Shooting in Felix's loft. (left to right) Lynch, Maslany, as Helena, Manson, and crew [1.04]

because the way the show is set up, there are clones, and they all have their different worlds," Welland explains. "There's Alison's world, there's Rachel's world, there's Sarah's world – everyone has a specific world. So it's unlike another show, where they all hang out at a coffee shop or something," Welland laughs.

Ian Brock was the *Orphan Black* production designer on Season One; John Dondertman joined between Seasons One and Two. "They set up different worlds for some of the main characters, so there were a few sets – Felix's and Alison's – that were established," Dondertman

says. "I didn't change any of that stuff, nor did we want to. It's not that uncommon in series for designers and D.P.s and directors to [come and go from] shows. It's something any creative has to get used to. But that [second] year, we brought in Dyad, so that was a new set of sets, and also the Proletheans, we brought that world in, which was the Johanssen farm."

Dondertman estimates that "In my immediate department, I have five people, but also in set dec[oration], there are at least twelve, there are thirty in the construction department, three or four in props. There are over fifty to sixty people

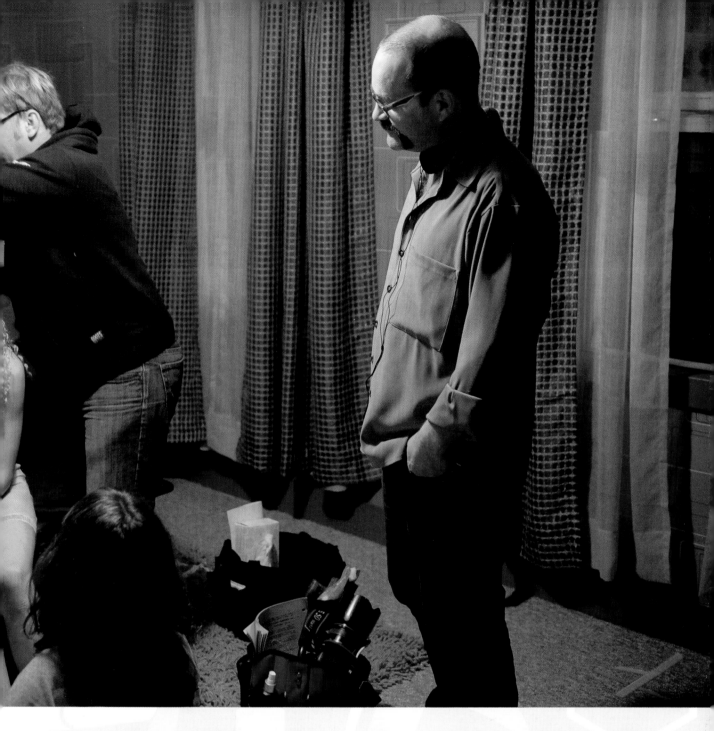

overall in my department – set design, set dec, props, construction and paint, locations."

"All of our sets have what we call 'wild walls,'" art director Jody Clement explains. "Wild walls are ways to shoot from a spot in the set that normally you would not be able to shoot in if you were in an actual building. For example, how many times have you seen people reaching into the refrigerator, and you have the point of view of looking from inside the refrigerator, looking out as the door opens? [To do that,] we would remove the walls to the set, and then we also cut a hole in the back of the refrigerator. The same

thing in the bathroom when they're washing their hands in the sink and they look in the mirror. When you have the point of view of the mirror looking at the actor, that would be a wall that's been taken out, and the camera is put in place. So wild walls happen all over our standing sets, which is one of the important things about actually having sets in the studio – you have the ability to shoot from above if you remove the ceiling, shoot from an angle that you can't normally get if you were in an actual building."

The Dyad Institute building has an unusual structure, with an upper floor that extends out

> ## *"It's the best compliment I could ever receive when an actor says, 'I know who I am now and I didn't when I sat down in the [makeup] chair.'"*

over the lower floor. "That's an existing location," Dondertman explains. "John Fawcett really liked that, so we designed the set to fit-match that building. Dyad is meant to be a mega-pharmaceutical drug and genetics company, so it did need to be state of the art."

However, Dyad has a second part. "There was an old building, which was actually a jail in Toronto, I think it goes way back to the early 1900s," says Dondertman. "We incorporated that, so there were old and new elements to that set. Cosima's lab in theory was in the restored old part of the building, and Leekie's office was in the brand-new part."

Cosima's lab is perhaps a little more interesting-looking than a real genetics lab would be. Dondertman concedes, "The one thing you

would have had in that lab is a DNA sequencer, which we never had. We did a lot of computers and monitors, and we put in a lot of lights to create a visual element. We do our research to try and make it feel real, but the real world is often not that photo-friendly. It can be kind of bland and uninteresting-looking, so we have to create our own version of reality. And that's like any TV show, be it a law show, cop show, doctor show, they all do similar tricks. For instance, in Dyad, we had a server tower. We have a guy who is a bit of an electronics whiz, and he puts in all the blinky lights and sequences the lights, so you see something there that makes it look good. Again, we do research it, so it still looks kind of real, but has a little bling on camera.

"In the rendition camp, we had our own portable server for computers that we spent quite a bit of time building – it had little screens with drone footage and lots of lights. We don't necessarily always feature that, but we try to make stuff look as real as possible."

Clement observes, "Cosima, at the beginning, sees all the lab equipment, but then she personalizes her space by putting in little bohemian-style area carpets and a plush little

Left: Two of Felix's paintings and loft set dressing.
This Image: Rachel and Dr. Leekie in his office [2.07]

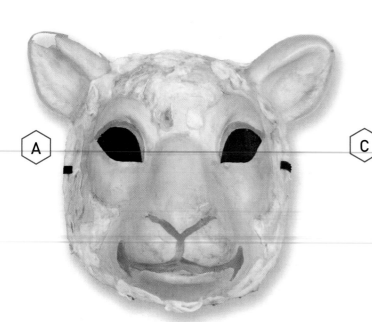

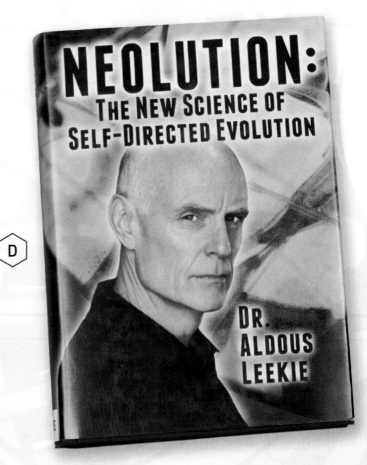

A) M.K.'s Dolly the Sheep mask. B) M.K.'s lemon iced tea mix. C) Dyad Institute key card. D) Dr. Aldous Leekie's book about Neolution. E) Kira's beloved sock monkey. F) M.K.'s backpack. G + H) P.T. Westmoreland's secretly influential text, with an illustration of Leda and the swan. I) Rachel's eyepatch

This Image: The crew prepping to shoot in the police station meeting room. **Right:** Rudy reports to Coady in one of the rendition camp trailers [3.03]. **Bottom Right:** Design schematic for the rendition camp prison cells

> "We do our research to try and make it feel real, but the real world is often not that photo-friendly. It can be kind of bland and uninteresting-looking, so we have to create our own version of reality."

sofa, a love seat, and a really cool lamp above her desk, something that would maybe be more suited for residential than office-like. It's got a lot of holes in it. You can see the light bulb inside and the structure itself, like it has twigs stacked around it to make a transparent lampshade."

Dyad also has a cell where Sarah is held prisoner. "That room is an idea John [Fawcett] had," Dondertman recalls. "It's black plexi, so in effect, it's black mirror. Actually, it's hard to see yourself – it still creates a reflection and creates a lot of depth, but it's not like a mirror-mirror, where you see everything. You can hide the crew and the camera in the mirror because it's black.

I suggested doing the floor-to-ceiling rear-projection screen on it, so it becomes a bit of a kaleidoscopic box. That was one of the favorite things I built that year. The corridors outside are all brick. The idea there is that that's part of the restored old part of Dyad, down in the dungeons."

An old edition of H.G. Wells' *The Island of Dr. Moreau* containing a hidden code plays a prominent part throughout the series. "We made it in the art department," Dondertman reveals. "We had an illustrator do a number of versions and we showed it to John and Graeme, and they picked something and we colorized it. We had to modify the interior as well, because of the code."

Clement adds, "Sasha [Kosovic], our art department apprentice, took the book home and doodled on every single page for an entire weekend, and created the symbols and the little sections."

Cosima's lab within Dyad has a warm feel, whereas other parts of Dyad look extremely cold. "It's not that we want them to look radically different," Dondertman explains, "but in Cosima's lab, in the old part, with these copper dark bronze columns and the brick, part of that [old jail] building we shot in had been restored

like that, so we lifted a lot of those details to match. That Cosima set is loosely based on one of the rooms in the old prison. So we carried the white through everything to tie it all together and make it feel like one environment, but as far as trying to make them feel different, it was really just working with the older and the newer parts of the building. In the floors [of Cosima's lab], there's stone tile, which we also matched to the location, and upstairs was marble to be in Leekie's office, the elevators, the lobby."

Dyad is run by, successively, Aldous Leekie, Rachel Duncan, Delphine Cormier, then Rachel again. "Leekie had his own artifacts in there that we took out," Dondertman points out. "He was a bit of an anthropology buff, so we had skulls and various anthropological artifacts in a glass case there. When Rachel took over for Leekie, it was the same office, minus some of his personal effects that we took out. With Delphine, we recreated the whole set, though we used some of the old set to do that."

Delphine's office aesthetic, Dondertman explains, is "clean contemporary. I used quite a bit of black and some wood. I tried to work towards quiet good taste, some elegance. I

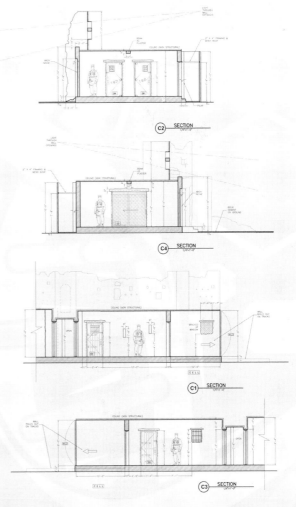

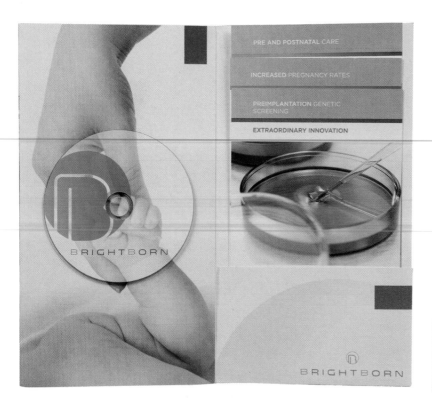

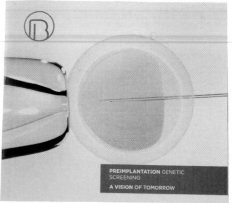

Pre and postnatal care

Increased pregnancy rates

Preimplantation genetic screening

Extraordinary innovation

Preimplantation genetic screening

A vision of tomorrow

BRIGHTBORN

MICRO-EXFOLIATING DERMA GEL

Deep Mineral Calming Cleanser

Soap-Free PH5.5 FORMULATED FOR SENSITIVE SKIN

250 mL - 6.76 FL.OZ.

BRIGHTBORN

HYDROLIPIDIC EMULSION

Lipid Enriched Restorative Cream

FORMULATED FOR SENSITIVE SKIN

225 mL - 7.6 FL.OZ.

BRIGHTBORN

TARGETED SKIN TONE CORRECTOR

Nutritive Deep Restorative Solution

FOR AGED AND TIRED SKIN

200 mL - 5.76 FL.OZ.

BRIGHTBORN

MINERAL INFUSED VITA-SOLUTION

Astringent Lotion

FOR ALL SKIN TYPES

160mL - 5.4 FL.OZ.

BRIGHTBORN

DERMO BARRIER REPAIR BALM

Restorative Formula

BRIGHTBORN
BRIGHTBORN

> *"We had a real one and we had a cast of a scorpion. So we moved between the real one and the fake one, but there was no CG work, so Tatiana was in the box with the real scorpion at times."*

always find black and wood look really good together, classic, like an old Jag, with the black leather and the wood. So we worked with that. In Leekie's office, I had a lot of wood in the ceiling and the walls, and I actually used that again, but we painted it. I found some new flooring for Delphine, some real marble for cost. We used a lot of glass as well. Everything pivots on a gymbal, so that if you're seeing a camera, you can turn the glass [so that the camera is no longer reflected in the shot]. We like to use reflections and shoot through glass for the Dyad part."

For the Prolethean compound, "The Johanssen ranch was based on a Mennonite environment," Dondertman says. "It's a cooperative religious group, living together on a farm. We had the basement lab, which Johanssen was doing his operations in, which was meant to be a converted lab that they would have treated the horses and cattle in previously. So that was a fun thing to make. They had Helena and Gracie stashed away [in what] would have been animal stalls. The rest of the house was all white clapboard."

The police station that is the workplace of Detective Art Bell (and the late Beth Childs) is meant to be the same in Seasons One and Four, but Dondertman reveals that changes have been made. "It's the same space, but we wanted a big corridor, so I created a corridor. They wanted different environments to work in. We're not using any of the same rooms, we're not using the main area, but it's got to feel like the same world. We've gone for almost an old New York-style precinct, with the black-and-white cars and the old-style badge on the plate."

As *Orphan Black* shoots primarily in Toronto,

the production team had to be creative when finding locations to look like the Mexican desert for shooting the rendition camp and cantina scenes. "The Castor camp itself is in the studio," Dondertman relates. "The exterior stuff, where Helena's running around and the jeeps are driving, that's in a gravel pit at the north end of the city." The footage was treated in post-production to make the hues more yellow and orange.

"And then we had the shipping containers – that's where the offices were, where [Virginia Coady's] office was – and we built those. A real container is too small to shoot in, so we built our own versions that were slightly larger. I welded up a whole frame, bought all the corrugated metal, so the walls could come off and we could shoot in them."

Coady's office has photos of the Castor clones in boyhood. As Dondertman explains, "The Castor brothers are self-aware, they knew about each other, so we created these photos, using actual photos of the actor [Ari Millen], and making

it look like they were different personalities, different kids, hanging out together."

When Helena is being held in the rendition camp, she interacts a lot with a scorpion. "We had a real one and we had a cast of a scorpion," Dondertman reveals. "So we moved between the real one and the fake one, but there was no CG work, so Tatiana was in the box with the real scorpion at times. They made sure it can't sting anybody or bite you or pinch you." However, it was the fake one that went into Maslany's mouth. "There might have been a little CG movement added to that."

There are a variety of challenges on *Orphan Black*, Dondertman notes. "The show is extremely detailed. There's a lot going on all the time, there's nothing really very simple or straightforward about any of it. In that first episode of Season Two, ["Nature Under Constraint and Vexed,"] we did quite a few sets. There was a bathroom that Sarah kicks her way out of and crawls through the hole. So we built that." In order to avoid injuring the performers, "It's drywall, and we used balsa wood, we used soft material, and then it's a combination of the actor and the stunt person. That was on the stage.

"When you see it on the screen, when you believe it to be true, there's a lot of work that goes into everything to make it that way."

We built the bathroom, so we had to sandwich the back of that diner, which was a practical location, into the interior design of the diner set, and then as you come around the hall end of the door, you match both sides of that in the studio, so that all connects, and it's quite seamless."

When creating Bubbles, the soap store owned by Alison's mother that the Hendrixes buy as a front for their drug operation, Dondertman recalls, "[The producers] said, 'Don't hold back, it should be over the top.' So we did the pink and purple stripes in there, and a lot of pink and lime green and we used all these glass bubbles we found and made the light fixtures out of them. That was quite an operation. We had to make all of the soap, because it couldn't be scented, as the crew can't work in an environment [with overwhelming scent]. We made five thousand bars of soap. Two weeks before Christmas, we found two or three small boutique soap makers, so they wouldn't be stretched too thin, to make it all. We just said, 'Make them look the same, but we can't have any scent at all.' The soap shop was tricky, just because we had to get all that product made, plus we had to make all the labels and create the graphic identity of the store."

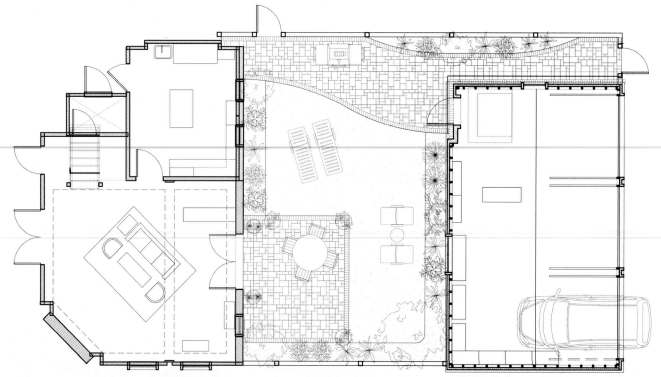

PLAN
Scale: 3/16"=1'-0"

Clockwise from Above: The apartment of Shay (Ksenia Solo), with Cosima [3.08]. The same area as it was originally, dressed as Felix's stairwell. Design schematic for the Hendrix house set. Signage concepts for the comic book store. The Hendrix house living room and backyard

When Cosima becomes romantically involved with Shay Davidov (Ksenia Solo) mid-way through Season Three, Dondertman enjoyed adapting an old set into the new character's apartment. "I converted Felix's stairwell, where Cal comes up the stairs to fight one of the Castors [in "Transitory Sacrifices of Crisis"], into Shay's. I took the staircase out, painted it all white, added some doors, some windows, and that became Shay's loft. I just roll from one set to the other."

Clement has been both a set designer (Season Two) and an art director (Seasons Three and Four) on *Orphan Black*. "It's been my favorite show to shoot," she says. "The production designer comes up with the concept and design for the sets and the look of the show. Then the art director takes that concept and helps implement it and makes sure that the departments – construction, props, set decorators, and then the people that work within the art department, the graphic designers, the set designer, and then any assistants to the art department – implement the goals of the production designer. Art director is more of a management job. You do have to have that creative background in order to become an art director, [but] it ends up becoming more of a management job. You have to speak the creative language, and be able to serve that

"The show is extremely detailed. There's a lot going on all the time, there's nothing really very simple or straightforward about any of it."

creative vision with the production designer, so that you can communicate to all of the other departments how to achieve what the production designer requires."

Kristian Bruun, who plays Donnie Hendrix, says he feels "a bit of ownership" when it comes to the Hendrix house sets. "We've spent a lot of crazy time in that garage. The backyard is actually quite cozy. It's pretty funny – it could be the middle of winter, but you go [into the soundstage], the backyard is there, the grass is green, you can sit out with the lights on in the studio, it's like the sun. So I love to sit in the backyard and read a book or do a crossword while they're setting up the next scene. So yeah, I do feel some weird kind of ownership of that house.

"I also love Felix's loft," Bruun adds. "That set has been next door to ours, so if we're using the Hendrix house, a lot of times, we'll be sitting in Felix's loft, just hanging out between scenes as they set up. That loft is so cool. It's so grungy and dirty and arty.

"There's also the set of a comic book store, which I absolutely love. It's filled with comics and games and figurines. It's fun to poke your head around and look at everything that they filled this store with, because it's filled with everything an authentic comic book store is.

"I love exploring all the sets," Bruun concludes, "because every drawer has something in it, and it's a totally realized environment that we can use as actors. Sometimes on other [shows'] sets, they're like, 'Oh, that doesn't move, so don't use that, and don't use that,' but here, we can completely be comfortable within the sets to fully use them and it's amazing how real they are. They do such a bang-up job with it."

A large portion of the visual effects work on *Orphan Black* is dedicated to its defining aspect: the clones. The show uses a specialized apparatus, the technodolly, to shoot scenes that feature more than one clone, though executive producer Claire Welland explains, "It wasn't created for us. It was an existing piece of equipment. We went to White's [William F. White International Inc.] and they had it. It's a form of motion control. They had to rewrite some software, because we were doing moves that it had never done before, and last year, we had some problems with it remembering a programmable move, so it had to be fixed, but most of the time, it's worked very well."

Geoff Scott is the visual effects supervisor on *Orphan Black* and is also senior visual effects supervisor at Intelligent Creatures, the company responsible for the show's visual effects. Intelligent Creatures has been involved with *Orphan Black* since before production began on Season One, Scott reports. "I met with John Fawcett and Claire Welland. We, our [Intelligent Creatures] art director and our CG supervisor, did a couple of film tests. We presented a couple of ideas on how to [do multi-clone shots]. We had one person put sugar in another person's coffee, and the other person then drank it, and then another test where we had [one clone] look like he was pushing himself up against a wall. That secured us the job, the fact that we showed up having a good understanding of what we needed to do. And that test of the one clone pushing the other one against the wall ended up working its way into the story, where Alison pushes Sarah up against the wall in Season One."

Scott explains, "When we first do a clone shot, I'll usually stick with the episode director, and we create a storyboard of the clone scenes. Often,

we'll create a top-down game plan, similar to football, 'This person's here, this person's here, camera will be here and moves through there,' so we have an overview of where we need everything to be. We present that to Aaron Morton, the cinematographer, and we plan out all the gags [bits of onscreen business]. For example, almost every clone scene, there's a point of physical contact [between clones]. We make sure we know what that is going to be, and when it's going to happen, and roughly where the camera is going to be. So when we present it, we tell Tat, 'You'll be here, and we'll need you to pass the object to [clone double] Kathryn Alexandre, and she'll need to take it with the upstage hand – the hand that's furthest away from camera – so Kathryn's hand will be onscreen when it's you as that other clone [in the final shot].' We rehearse it, and then we adjust the camera. Aaron has a better eye for picking camera angles and heights than I do. And Tatiana always makes the

Left: Alexandre as Helena, rescuing Maslany as Sarah [2.04]. **Top Right:** Alexandre as Beth, Maslany as M.K. **Right:** Roles reversed, Alexandre as M.K. and Maslany as Beth [4.01].

Maslany as Sarah, Vokey, Maslany as Cosima
in a final shot of 2 clones touching [4.02]

> *"Tatiana always makes the characters come to life, so she's always adding to the performance, making it better."*

characters come to life, so she's always adding to the performance, making it better. Then, once we've rehearsed it, an hour before we go to shoot, we bring in the technodolly."

"The technodolly is basically like a small camera crane that has a telescoping arm and runs like a dolly on a track," John Fawcett says, "but it's all computer controlled. So the camera sits on that, and it all runs from and feeds into a big computer."

"It's essentially a motion-controlled fifteen-foot crane arm that will completely repeat the same move once we decide what it needs to do and walk it through its paces and time it out," Scott

elaborates. "We make sure that Tatiana starts the scene as the clone that is motivating the camera moves. Once we've shot a pass that we like of her in that role, we run it a couple more times, but with the acting double [taken] out." Audio from the double's earlier take is used on playback for timing. "We shoot a couple more times with Tatiana as the first clone," Scott continues. "Then we lock the set down, Tatiana goes and changes into the next clone, and her acting double changes into the clone that Tatiana previously was. As often as we can, they're in the scene together, so that Tatiana can get a sense of who the other person is, the amount of space she takes up, somebody to act against."

When, for instance, Alison hands a cup of tea to Sarah, while Maslany will play both characters in the final sequence, it may be Alexandre's arm holding the teacup if we see Maslany-as-Sarah as the shot's primary focus. Scott says, "What we'll do often is, we'll have Tat move her

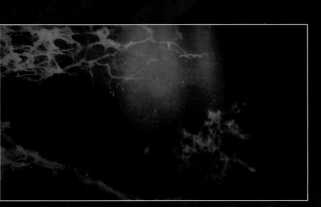

Orphan Black's idiosyncratic opening titles are visual effects, but what exactly are we seeing? John Fawcett reveals, "Graeme and I got fascinated with the biochemistry of slime molds, and how they replicate and duplicate. It was something that felt like thematically it worked [for *Orphan Black*]. So that sort of was the genesis of it – one of the main components is slime mold videos."

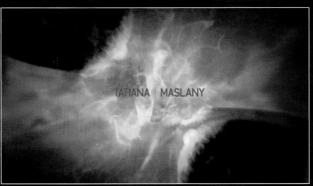

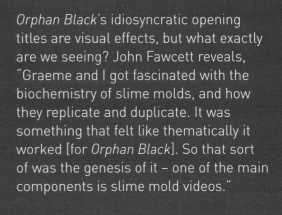

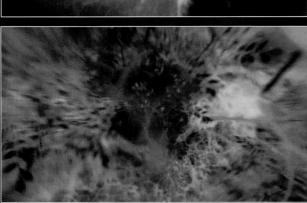

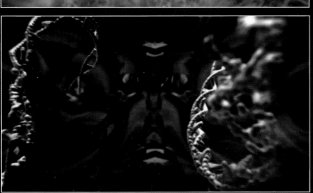

> "We create a storyboard of the clone scenes. Often, we'll create a top-down game plan... so we have an overview of where we need everything to be."

shoulder to sell the movement across the body. If you move your arm, your shoulder moves, your hips shift. There's a transfer of weight that is almost unconscious. We make sure that Tat does all of that, and then we take Kathryn's arm and we anchor it in place. We will have Tat mime the action, but her shoulder [moves] in the timing of when Kathryn has moved [her arm]. We'll isolate Kathryn's arm sometimes. There's a timing of the motion so it lines up with what both Tat and Kathryn did, and we'll tweak it."

This is, Scott relates, a very sophisticated version of a traditional film technique known as split screen. "Where we push it to the next level is, we move the camera with motion control, as opposed to locking the camera off, and then run what would be a traditional split screen. Also, generally, in a more traditional split screen, [the clones would be] separated, no crossover, no passing of objects."

Even when there are more than two clones in a shot, the screen will only be split into two

areas. "We usually have about an hour or more between clones, for wardrobe, hair and makeup to work their magic," Scott says, "so in that time, we do a very rudimentary composite of the clone scene, and then we bring in the third clone on the single-screen split."

The computer doesn't do the work of removing Alexandre's face and putting in Maslany's. "It's the artists who do it," Scott reveals. "They use a process called rotoscoping, and they will hand cut-out a hand or an arm, or whatever piece they need to isolate from Tatiana. They'll zoom right down to a blurry pixel level, and they will start isolating all those pieces by hand. We have a team of literally the best people doing this now in the world."

Developing the best technique for shooting with the technodolly has been a process of trial and error from the start. Scott recalls the first clone scene the company attempted to shoot. "John Fawcett and myself primed it for a few weeks. It was when Tatiana as Sarah, pretending to be Beth, met Katja in the car. It was supposed

to be a relatively calm, overcast day. And then as the day progressed, the sky turned black as this storm rolled in, the winds picked up to about eighty kilometers an hour, and it started torrentially downpouring, which is the worst-case scenario, because we have this incredibly expensive technodolly out there. So then Aaron, the cinematographer, had to start bringing in lights. At one point, the tarp that was brought in to block the rain that was going sideways was so full of water that somebody tipped it to tip the water out [and] the water poured into the mechanism of the technodolly. It didn't want to work for about twenty minutes. It finally decided it was going to work, but for the rest of the day, it made this horrible grinding, crunching noise. We sat there, got the footage. I had to [digitally] isolate Katja out of all of her footage and place her into the footage of Sarah, because otherwise, it was so dark that, even with all the work Aaron had done, it still looked like nighttime by the time we were done. So from that point forward,

we decided that we were never going to do a two-clone shot outdoors ever again."

This is why sets like the Hendrix backyard and the rendition camp are built on soundstages. The sky and backgrounds are created within the computers of Intelligent Creatures, where the visual effects unit working on *Orphan Black* varies between three and thirty people. "We have a matte painting team here," Scott says. "Digital painting, but it's the same level of artistry [as paintings made on canvas]. For the rendition camp, the [CG set] extensions are created by three different matte painters that we have in-house, and what we use is dependent on the type of shot it is. We'll sometimes take that matte painting, we project it onto three-dimensional geometry, so that we can then track it into 3D space, and it moves accurately, with the right amount of parallax, and then we composite it into the shot. For the rendition camp, we had a bluescreen around it. In the Hendrix backyard, we had bluescreen off to the other side of it. We

This Image: The set-up for the celebratory sestras (and loved ones) dinner party at Bubbles, with the technodolly track in the foreground [3.10]. **Opposite:** Maslany as Helena, Bailey Corneal as Alison, Heidi Malley as Cosima, Alexandre as Sarah

> **"[The technodolly]'s essentially a motion-controlled fifteen-foot crane arm that will completely repeat the same move once we decide what it needs to do..."**

take our aesthetic direction based on what Aaron Morton has lit the scene for."

Some characters require special considerations. Helena, for instance, must be shot with bluescreen rather than greenscreen, because of her yellow hair. "Green is made up of yellow and blue, so we found that we were working much harder to isolate her [yellow] hair from the greenscreen," Scott explains. "Season Two, we switched entirely from greenscreen to bluescreen, and have had incredible results."

Scott often has input into the technical side of the work and is always on set for the clone scenes. "In rehearsal, Tat and I will find ourselves touching each other, or gesturing in a certain way," Alexandre relates, "and then we'll look at Geoff and say, 'Is this possible?' And he'll indicate yes or no. And then, usually after the first take, Geoff will say, 'Try and lean more to your left on this mark,' or, 'I'm going to be using your right arm, so make sure you place it right here,' or, 'Your right arm won't exist in the final edit, so keep it behind your back.' Every day, it's things like that."

Maslany says of the clone scenes, "It's a constant struggle in a way, because it is such

a creative job, but at the same time, if I don't hit that mark, and if I don't make sure that I'm looking at that eye-line, then it doesn't fly, we don't believe it. So there's a cool mix of the two things. I actually really enjoy that mix, trying to find spontaneity and surprise in the extremely technical thing of the clone scenes. But it also becomes part of the job, and so as we get better at it, I think I just get braver with how we challenge it. By this point, we've done four-clone scenes, we've done four clones and five [non-clone] people over for dinner, so we're always pushing the boundaries of what we're willing to try."

Regarding acting double Kathryn Alexandre, Maslany enthuses, "I'm so lucky to have Kathryn, because she's an amazing actor, and also technically so intuitive and so smart, and she does so much work to show up every day prepared with ideas and questions. She really has complete ownership over these characters as far as I'm concerned. She's fully helped me create them, whether it's her doing something in a scene that inspires me to take it into my side of that scene – she's improvised things as Helena that then I've gone and replicated when I'm playing Helena – or she's asked me questions, because there's only so much I can keep in my head, and she'll sometimes come up with a question that puts me back on track, and is so helpful. She watches all of the dailies, so that when she comes to set, she has all of the dialogue, the dialect, the character's movement, the instincts of the character down, and she's able to give me a complete performance."

Alexandre explains, "I always play one

character before Tat does in a particular scene. So sometimes she can give me a rough idea of how she wants that character to move throughout the scene, but a lot of it is guesswork for me, and that's where all of that research that I've done behind the scenes comes into play, because I have to think about what the character wants, and how they just move in that scene. Hopefully, I do it close to what she ends up doing, but it's never going to be a hundred percent. So it's much easier when I'm playing the character that she's already played, and there can be more mimicry at that point."

Sometimes there are other characters in the scenes with multiple clones, Alexandre adds. "It's always interesting to have another actor come into those situations, and [see them] have to learn the beast. They often have to play opposite me, as opposed to Tat, which also puts

Top: Maslany as Alison, acting opposite a tennis ball standing in for Sarah. **Above:** Maslany as both Alison and Sarah in the completed shot [2.07]. **Opposite Top:** Soundstage marks on the floor for camera moves and performers for the clone dance party. **Opposite Bottom:** The clone dance as it's assembled on the set monitor [2.10]

"It is such a creative job, but at the same time, if I don't hit that mark, and if I don't make sure that I'm looking at that eye-line, then it doesn't fly, we don't believe it."

extra onus on me to really be there as an actor for them, and to not just be mimicking her, even though I have to get [her] as bang-on as I can."

"It is a very patient, technical, precise process of working," Kristian Bruun observes. "I actually kind of like it, because it's so anal retentive. Everything has to be timed perfectly, the length of the scene has to be the same, the timing you say the lines has to be the same, the places you move within the scene have to be the same, the height of your hand as you reach for something has to be the same at the same time as it was done in previous scenes. Sometimes you're working with a tennis ball at eye level [so that the gaze will be in the right place], sometimes you're working with a body double, sometimes you're working with nobody there, sometimes you're faking eye lines. It's one of the most technically demanding acting jobs I've ever had, and it's so exciting to do, because when you get it right, it's so incredible and it's such a relief as you slowly get through the scene and adjust with every take," he laughs.

"Tat and Kathryn are really something else. They are incredible to watch. They've become so in tune with each other, with each other's mannerisms, and what Tat's going to do as another clone, Kathryn's going to [anticipate], and it's brilliant to watch them work, and then getting the privilege to do a scene with them is just a bonus on top of that."

Kevin Hanchard relates, "I think the repetition serves to help you a little bit. It does become quite taxing, but the more takes you have – up until a certain point, anyway – it allows you to understand the scene more, it allows you to get deeper into your body, and you just get more familiar and you act less, if that makes sense.

You just are, which is sort of the state that you want to be in, especially when you're on camera. When you're on stage, you have to hit the back of a big eight-hundred-seat auditorium, and you have to emote a little more, whereas in film and television, you just have to think the thoughts and trust that that's enough. So when we do those technodolly scenes, where it's eight hours, ten hours of doing the same scene, after a while, you know the scene so well that you just have to listen to your partner and let that be enough, and trust that the thoughts that you're thinking will make their way through into the camera."

Jordan Gavaris sums it up. "When it works, it's great. When it doesn't work, we all just want to throw ourselves off a cliff."

Fawcett describes shooting a multi-clone scene. "Let's say it's Sarah, Alison and Cosima. Usually, prior to getting to set, we've had some rehearsal time. So we'll bring in Tat, we'll bring in Kathryn Alexandre, who is Tat's acting double, and then we have a couple of other girls that we use if we're doing more than two clones.

So we'll have those three, we'll block it like a normal scene, and if Tat wants to play Sarah to begin with, she can play Sarah, Kathryn can play Alison, and the other girl can play Cosima. We'll block the scene, work through it. I'll usually have my cinematographer there and we'll talk about the kind of shots we're envisioning, what parts we're going to cover with the motion-control unit, and what parts we're going to shoot just in the coverage. When I say 'coverage,' I mean, here's a close-up of Sarah over [the shoulder of] Alison [who has her back to camera]. Those kinds of shots are simple, because you could just do a close-up of Tat playing Sarah over Kathryn playing Alison, and you never see Kathryn's face.

The clone shots are where we're trying to see Tatiana and Tatiana and Tatiana all in the same shot, and moving around in space, and where the camera is moving about and tracking them. So all that stuff gets locked in a rehearsal with three girls, so you can literally see three people in the same place.

"When we get to set, we'll have the same three people there, show the crew the blocking, and we'll start shooting with all three girls," Fawcett continues. "We will shoot it like you shoot any normal shot. The crew operates the camera, they pull focus, the dolly guys push the dolly. We do it until the shot's right. We go, 'Okay, that was perfect, that's what we're going

This Image: Maslany Sestras Unite! Alexandre as Sarah, Maslany as Helena, Corneal as Alison, Malley as Cosima, costumed for Helena's baby shower dream [3.01]. **Right:** Corneal as Alison, Maslany as Sarah, Gavaris, Alexandre as Helena, Wexler, Malley as Cosima, and crew members

> ## "Tat and Kathryn are really something else. They are incredible to watch. They've become so in tune with each other, with each other's mannerisms..."

to slave to.' So this is our hero camera move. From there on out, the camera is going to repeat that same action, we're going to build layers, and the camera is just going to repeat, over and over and over again, that same move. If Tat is playing Sarah first, we'll want to cut out her lines where she is playing Sarah, so she can only hear the off-camera lines. The procedure would be, after we've got the shot set with the

three girls, we'll put an ear wig in Tatiana's ear, where she's hearing the off-camera lines, but those [other] girls are no longer on set. So she has to look at tennis balls and remember where each girl was, and where she's got to look, and then put her dialogue in, and she's hearing the feed lines coming in to her ear. Once that Sarah layer is done, there might be some coverage to the scene that needs to get shot. Then you send Tat away, she'd change, become Alison, and then you would be doing exactly the same thing, cutting all the lines out except for the Alison lines, running with all three girls in to get her back into the rhythm of it, but then taking those girls away and just repeat the camera moves until you get right to the end, and it's probably super-late by that time, and everyone's practically in tears because they're so tired, and you let them finally, at the end of the day, look at

your little gift, which is, you can see all the layers occurring on the monitor, all at the same time, and you can see what you've done for the day."

Scott cites the "clone dance party" as the most challenging sequence for the visual effects department. "Because it was our first four-clone shot, we had to figure out how we could do it. It required, I think, over twenty hours of meetings and rehearsals and prep before we shot a thing. And then it was very specific, because of who was tied to which portion of the take. We threaded Felix as our bridge. So at a certain point, every time he jumps, he'll leave shot for a frame. We started with Felix attached to Cosima when they're dancing. Then he left frame, came back in. We then filmed him separately with Tatiana as Alison. Then we had him just scoot past Helena, and we locked her into an area, which we'd marked out on the floor, saying,

'Please, you have to stay inside this box.' Once he left frame, his job was done, so Tat came back as Sarah, and then we had him come in from the other side of frame, and then he was physically interacting with her. That one took a lot of choreography, because we had essentially five moving bodies in the shot.

"The dinner was its own separate set of challenges, because we had so many moving parts," Scott continues. "We had a full dinnerware set, we had speeches, we had people passing stuff to each other. One saving grace was, we were able to get Grant Kilroy, our carpenter, to lock the chairs down. So we at least knew that the person in this seat is going to be the person who's sitting in this seat. That helped immensely. But not only did we have four clones, we had five additional people in the clone scene. So technically, it was a nine-person clone scene."

Orphan Black has a worldwide fan following known as the Clone Club. Miriam Salzman is one of three co-runners of the New York chapter. "On social media, it's astounding," says Salzman. "I have tons of friends that I've made, all over the world, because of the show."

When Salzman meets someone who doesn't know about *Orphan Black*, "I tell people about the acting. You go for the acting, and you stay for the story, you stay for everything else. And Clone Club, the fandom, is such a creative community. It's such a family that this show has brought together."

Executive producer Kerry Appleyard says she's delighted by how *Orphan Black* "has resonated so well with fans of all ages. It's being hailed not just as a Canadian success, but it's up there with the big successful shows of the past few years, and also the critical acclaim that Tatiana's got, the Emmy, for this weird little show. We all knew we had something special, but we didn't know how much it was going to resonate."

Maria Doyle Kennedy says the fandom "totally surprised me." Over the years of doing panels at San Diego Comic-Con, "We moved from these relatively small rooms to these gigantic, stadium-sized rooms. And then when the lights came up on the back half of the room, it was actually twice as big as we thought it was. Seeing it grow so exponentially like that, that's incredible. And then some of the stories that people share at the conference, quite personal experiences, are really amazing. In my teens, I would connect to people through shared love of bands. Only I grew up in Ireland. It's an island, it's a small place.

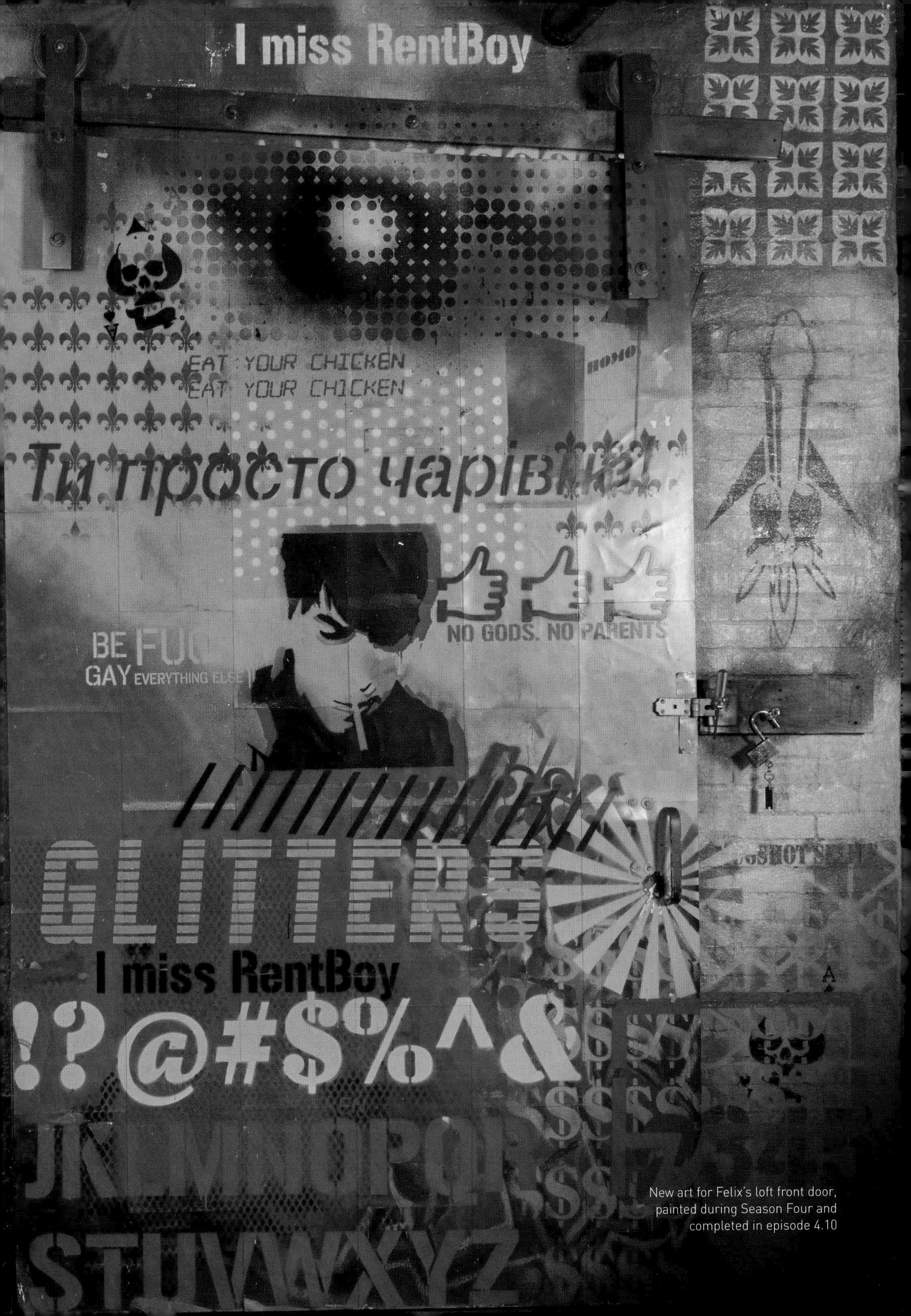

I miss RentBoy

EAT YOUR CHICKEN
EAT YOUR CH1CKEN

Ти просто чарівне!

BE FUC
GAY EVERYTHING ELSE

NO GODS. NO PARENTS

GLITTER$

I miss RentBoy

!?@#$%^&

New art for Felix's loft front door,
painted during Season Four and
completed in episode 4.10

It's not easy to find your people. [With Clone Club], you see these people bonding over their shared love for the show, and they've already been talking to each other before online, and you see them coming like they're finding their tribe. It's quite joyful to us."

"Twitter is my main method of connecting with the fans," Kevin Hanchard says. "I also go on Tumblr, which is where they post so much of the fan art. There's so much out there, and it's so varied, and it's so diverse, so much talent, and they're using it to talk about what we do. It's the kind of stuff that I would put on my wall, portraits of me and of Tatiana that we have up in the studio and in the production office, that are gallery worthy. I think we've got some of the best fans in the world. They come in every age, shape, sex. I love them."

At conventions, Hanchard adds, "It's great when you get out there and you see a thousand people lined up for two hours to meet you. It makes you realize that you're affecting people. As an actor, what more could you ask for?"

Kristian Bruun agrees. "The fans are very caring, very active online members. They've been so good at growing the show – they're the perfect marketers. They make us want to do a good job for them, because they are so supportive. It's really quite wonderful to see."

"I think it's been the most surprising and rewarding thing about the whole experience for all of us," Graeme Manson says of the fan reaction, "that Tatiana has managed to strike a chord with so many people, particularly young women. The incredible creativity of the fans has been a joy for us. I just hope that when we wrap it up it feels like this logical end to the story, but that Clone Club will continue to live on."

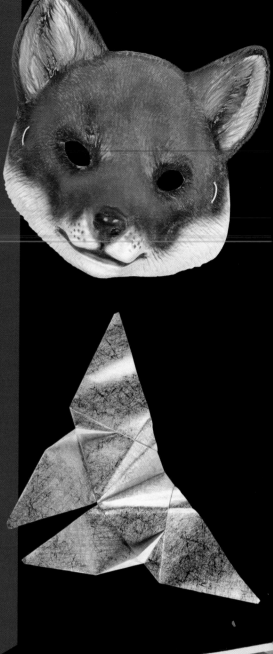

THE
CLONE CLUB
IS PROUD TO PRESENT

THE BEST ACTRESS IN THE WORLD AWARD

To the beautiful

TATIANA GABRIELLE MASLANY

For her outstanding performance and lead role in "ORPHAN BLACK",
strength, Cosima's intelligence, Helena's soft side, Alison's crazy ideas
making us fall in love with each and every single

Dear Neighbour,

I'm a mom of two school-aged children who believes every child deserves the same shot at a quality public education.

As a long time resident of Glendale, **I believe our schools should be the heart of our community**. Our schools deserve a trustee with energy, drive and experience—a trustee who is engaged in our community, answers your calls and works with you to find solutions for our children.

Working together we can:

✓ I will put your family's educational interests first.
✓ I'll work to improve our academic achievement scores
✓ I will attend Parent Council Meetings, gather feedback & lend a hand.
✓ Listen and consult with all members of the public school committee.

Now is the time for strong leadership in the ward and the Glendale School District. I hope I can count on your support.

**VOTE FOR ALISON
VOTE FOR CHANGE**

**Alison HENDRIX
SCHOOL TRUSTEE**

GLENDALE SCHOOL TRUSTEE CANDIDATE

Far Left, Top to Bottom: The "stupid" fox mask Beth refuses to wear to talk to M.K. online [4.01]. Kira's origami angel [2.04]. Clone Club's award to Maslany. **Left, Top to Bottom:** Summer of String bracelets by Miriam Salzman on John, Graeme and Tatiana. Manson in his Time Vampire hardhat. One of Charlotte's paintings of the island. **Above, Top to Bottom:** The table read through for episodes 4.01 + 4.02. Lynch costumed for Halloween as Alison-costumed-as-Helena. The back of the postcard supporting Alison's School Board Trustee run

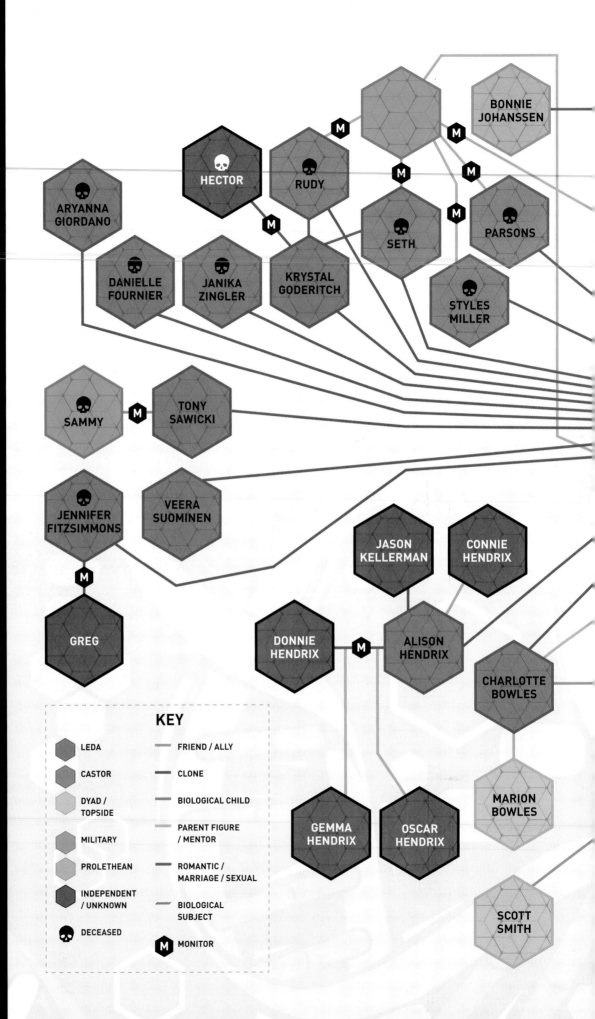

KEY

- LEDA
- CASTOR
- DYAD / TOPSIDE
- MILITARY
- PROLETHEAN
- INDEPENDENT / UNKNOWN
- DECEASED

- FRIEND / ALLY
- CLONE
- BIOLOGICAL CHILD
- PARENT FIGURE / MENTOR
- ROMANTIC / MARRIAGE / SEXUAL
- BIOLOGICAL SUBJECT
- M MONITOR

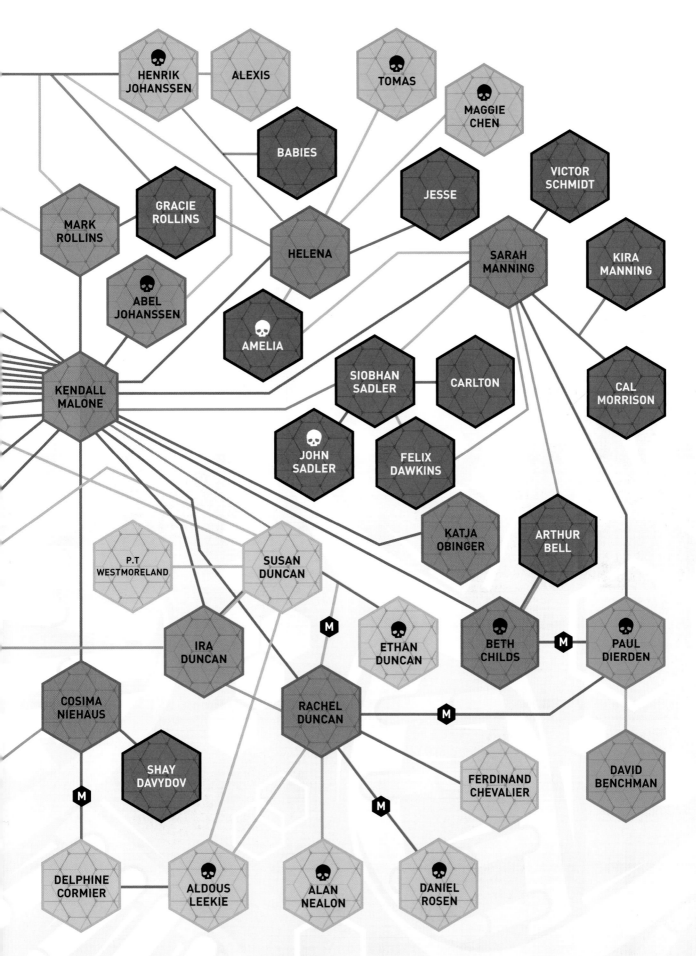

The author would like to thank (in alphabetical order) Kathryn Alexandre, Kerry Appleyard, Dylan Bruce, Kristian Bruun, Jessica Cail, Jody Clement, Laura Cobb, Russ Cochrane, Mackenzie Donaldson, John Dondertman, John Fawcett, Nicki Fioravante, Jordan Gavaris, Kevin Hanchard, Debra Hanson, Rachel Hunt, Maria Doyle Kennedy, Alex Levine, Stephen Lynch, Graeme Manson, Tatiana Maslany, Erin Masters, Curtis Matthews, Ari Millen, Rob Moden, Evan Moore, Carlos Pacheco, Miriam Salzman, Geoff Scott, Sandy Sokolowski, Juli Strader, Phoebe Trousdell, Rua Wani, Claire Welland, Pam Winter, Ruth Young, and my editors Jo Boylett and Nicola Edwards and designer Cameron Cornelius at Titan Books.